MYLOR

The Most Powerful Horse in the World

Michael Maguire

Illustrated by Nicholas Armstrong

A TARGET BOOK

published by

the Paperback Division of

W. H. ALLEN & Co. Ltd.

A Target Book
Published in 1977
by the Paperback Division of W. H. Allen & Co. Ltd
A Howard & Wyndham Company
44 Hill Street, London W1X 8LB

First published in Great Britain by
Allan Wingate (Publishers) Ltd, 1977

Printed in Great Britain by
Richard Clay (The Chaucer Press) Ltd, Bungay, Suffolk

ISBN 0 426 11877 4

ACKNOWLEDGEMENT

My special thanks to Nick Armstrong for
interpreting the story so well with his
marvellous illustrations

For my Mother
who taught me so much
about the quality of
life

Chapter One

'Zoot!' The word emerged from my sister's throat pretty forcefully. It was a favourite exclamation of hers and one she always used to voice her displeasure. 'It looks spooky and weird and unwelcoming,' she added. 'Who ever heard of anyone building a house in the middle of a maze?'

Poor Angel, whenever things didn't quite live up to the mental picture she'd built up in her mind she was swamped with disappointment. In this instance it was the name of a house. Parkway Grange. A name she'd conjured with over the past couple of weeks until a chocolate box image of an ivy-covered Devonshire manor house with latticed windows and sweeping lawns had emerged and stamped itself indelibly on her brain.

I struggled up to the gates with our suitcases and peered at the straggly blocks of privet hedges which wound away from us in all directions. It did look a little eerie and I had no idea how we were supposed to reach the house. We'd have to make for the centre and as I'd once tried to do that in the famous maze at Hampton Court Palace, I knew it to be no easy task. I tried not to let my thoughts show on my face. 'The Professor doesn't like uninvited visitors,' I said. 'He designed the maze as a way of keeping people out.'

'The taxi driver said Professor Parkway was eccentric. Doesn't that mean he's dotty?'

'Of course not.'

'Then what does it mean?'

'Well, it means...' I floundered.

'Yes, Roger?' Angel jammed her hands deep into the pockets of her jeans and narrowed her blue eyes.

'It means he's very clever and a little unusual, that's all. Most professors have diplomas and things to show they have brains. Dotty means mad. There's nothing mad about Professor Parkway.'

'Humph!' The tilt of her chin was defiant.

'And what's *humph* supposed to mean?'

'It means I'm not going to like it here. I wish I'd gone pony trekking. I always spend the Easter holidays riding on Dartmoor.'

'How boring.'

'I happen to enjoy it.'

'Don't you want real excitement?'

'I'm not a boy. I'm happy when I'm with horses.'

'Then you'll be happy here.'

'Does the Professor own horses?' She brightened visibly.

'Not exactly,' I hedged. 'Wait and see. I guarantee you're in for a surprise.'

'A nasty shock more like.' She threw me a swift, unsmiling glance.

'You're anticipating the worst. Boff invited us to his grandfather's house because the Professor needs our individual talents for a special project. We'll have a super time, you'll see.'

'A lot of my school friends think Boff's a little dotty,' Angel huffed, flicking strands of blonde hair away from her eyes.

'They're only jealous because he's very brainy,' I retaliated. I gave the big door handle a twist and the rusty hinges screamed as the gates parted.

'W-what's that?' Angel grabbed the sleeve of my leather jerkin and yanked me to a halt. The loud wail of a siren floated over the privet hedges. The noise was deafening.

8

I wrestled to control our little cairn terrier who was barking and tugging on his leash. 'Some sort of warning system,' I said and then I didn't say any more. My feet tangled with the leash and I fell clumsily to the ground.

'Spider's frightened!' Angel shrieked, clamping her hands to her ears. 'What a horrible way to start a holiday. Have you hurt yourself? Are you all right? Oh, do get up, Roger! Lying there isn't going to help!'

I hadn't adopted the flat-on-my-back position for my own comfort. Spider had weaved several loops around my ankles and I was having the devil's own job to get free. I managed it after a bit of effort and clambered shakily to my feet. As I began dusting myself down the piercing note of the siren gradually died.

'Sorry if the noise scared you.' Boff Parkway's amused voice boomed from a loudspeaker mounted high in a tree. 'When you opened the gate you broke the beam and triggered the mechanism. Stay where you are and I'll send transport to collect you.'

'I – we don't think this is very funny.' Angel whirled.

'Stop complaining, Angel,' Boff replied, still amused. 'I promise you're going to have the holiday of a lifetime.'

'You can hear me?' Angel's eyes widened in disbelief.

'Hear and see you. Look to the left of the loudspeaker and you'll see a closed-circuit TV camera.'

We both looked. A square lens glinted at us as it swivelled and was caught by the sun. A distant humming noise set Spider barking again, and as the noise got progressively louder he took refuge by hiding behind our suitcases.

9

'Mazemobile almost there,' Boff announced. 'Load yourselves and your luggage inside and I'll see you at the workshop.'

'Mazemobile?' Angel's eyes raked my face. 'What on earth is a mazemobile?'

I lifted and dropped my shoulders.

Boff explained. 'It's a small car that's been programmed to transport you safely through the maze to the house. All you have to do is remember the rhyme.' There was a metallic click as the loudspeaker was switched off.

I glanced at Angel. She was standing quite still, hands on hips and apparently tongue-tied. She looked almost boyish in her denims and white polo-necked sweater, but then she always did. She'd never been one for ribbon-and-lace prettyism.

'Rhyme?' she said softly, almost to herself. 'What rhyme? This is all becoming a childish game.'

'You're wrong, Angel,' I stated. 'It certainly isn't a game. We're here for a mission of great importance.'

'Well, I'll believe that when –' Her words skidded to a halt.

Spider jumped into my arms as the mazemobile rumbled out of a privet avenue, circled twice around us, parked neatly and sat silently staring at us. Yes, *staring*. It was shaped like a huge ladybird. Bright orange in colour with large black spots, small piercing eyes and antennae that were constantly on the move. Closer inspection revealed the spots to be tinted glass portholes which allowed me to see through to a plushly upholstered interior. Dials, knobs and electronic equipment were in great profusion. It was like something from a moonbase.

Angel looked dubious for a moment. 'There aren't any doors,' she said simply. 'How are we supposed –'

'The shell separates in the centre,' I interrupted,

spotting the join and working loose the spring-loaded clips which parted the two halves. 'Now you climb inside while I secure the luggage.'

She entered very gingerly, sat in the passenger seat and clutched Spider on her lap. I stowed our cases in the rear compartment and joined her. I clamped the shell shut and fastened the interior clips. We sat silently looking at each other, waiting for something to happen.

'We're not moving,' Angel remarked after a minute had elapsed.

'No sound from the motor,' I agreed.

'Perhaps you're supposed to push a button or something.'

'Boff didn't say so.'

'He knows Daddy's a pilot.'

'What's that got to do with it?'

'Well, he knows you're learning to fly. He's seen Daddy teaching you.'

'But this is nothing like an aircraft,' I protested. 'There's no joy-stick or steering –'

'Zoot!' Angel pointed a finger towards a panel on the dashboard. It had started to flash and words were beginning to appear.

> *I'll only obey if you remember my rhyme*
> *About the flames and the babies and the*
> *element of time.*

'Rhymes again,' Angel sighed in contempt. 'I told you it was childish. We have to say a nursery rhyme before we can move.'

'That's not childish, that's clever. The mazemobile won't react until it's fed the correct data. It's a sort of security precaution. Say the correct rhyme and the motor will respond.'

'I don't remember any rhymes,' she cupped her

chin in her hands and gave me a long, brooding look. 'I'm twelve years old, not a baby.'

'No, but you're behaving like one.'

'Don't be hateful!'

'Then try acting your age. I need your help to start the machine.'

'Oh, all right!' She sat up impulsively. 'It's easy – everybody knows the ladybird rhyme.'

'Then say it.'

'Now?'

'Yes, now.'

'Ladybird, ladybird, fly away home, your house is on fire and your children all gone.' She took a deep breath and glared. 'There, satisfied now?'

Certainly the machine was satisfied. Spider gave a nervous little bark as the motor rumbled into life. We were jerked back in our seats and suddenly my senses were deadened by the most stupendous roar as the mazemobile moved forward at incredible speed. The privet hedges were just a blur of greenery as we flashed past them. Left and right – right and left, so fast it was impossible to remember the route. As we rocked from side to side I could see the ladybird's antennae brushing the walls of the maze as if keeping it on course. We didn't have time to feel frightened. It was ten times better than any fairground ride and it was all over so quickly that it just left us breathless.

Angel peered wide-eyed through one of the portholes as we screeched to a halt. I could see she was brightening by the second. Parkway Grange was exactly how she'd envisaged it; all whitewash and timbers and covered in ivy. Beyond were low hills patterned by fields and meadows which rippled when caught by the wind. I unfastened the interior clips and separated the shell.

'Roger and Angel Young, I presume?' The voice

came from the side and it startled me. A big bony hand was thrust forward for me to shake. 'My grandson's told me so much about you, yes indeed. You're about the right height too. Climb out and let me have a proper look at you.'

Big humorous eyes smiled at me from behind spectacle lenses as thick as milk bottle glass. They eyed me up and down at considerable length and made me feel a little uneasy. Finally I said, 'Is my size of importance, sir?'

'Paramount, my boy. Absolutely paramount. How old are you?'

'Thirteen.'

'And not tall for your age.'

'If anything I'm a little on the short side.'

'So I can see. That's excellent. Yes, yes, indeed.'

'I'm almost as tall as Roger,' Angel broke in.

'Indeed you are, young lady. Rather pretty too if my eyes aren't deceiving me.'

'Why is it excellent, sir?' It was my turn to break in.

'Why is what excellent, Roger?'

'Me being on the short side.'

'Because of the project, my boy. You wouldn't fit you see.'

'Fit?'

'Fit into –' He stopped and began scratching the fringe of grey hair above his right ear. 'Hasn't my grandson told you?'

I shook my head. 'I only know that Angel and I have special talents which are important to you. I haven't a clue as to what they are or how you intend to use them.'

'Then you are in for a surprise. Oh, dear me. Yes, yes, indeed.'

He began chuckling in a very deep good-natured

We left the mazemobile and headed for the workshop. 'You are in for a surprise,' the Professor chuckled. 'Oh, dear me. Yes, yes, indeed.'

sort of way and his tartan waistcoat seemed to expand with every breath. He was rather big around the middle and I couldn't help thinking that all that extra wind would burst his buttons at any minute. Certainly his complexion got redder, his spectacles danced on the bridge of his nose, and he took on a decidedly froggy look as he blew out his cheeks.

'Is something funny, Professor?' Angel posed the question.

'I'm sorry, young lady.' He pulled a polka-dot handkerchief from his waistcoat and began mopping his brow. 'I'm laughing at myself, not at you. I'm a trifle absent-minded, you know. I was forgetting the need for absolute secrecy.'

'But now we're here –'

'Indeed. Yes, yes, indeed. All will be revealed quite soon.'

I was so confused that my sense of adventure was deserting me and all that accumulated excitement was ebbing away. 'I know it has something to do with a horse,' I advanced, 'so I can understand why you want Angel. But why you should want me...?'

'You're of prime importance, my boy. You have the experience you see.'

'No, I don't see. I know very little about horses.'

'But you know how to take off and land a light aircraft. You know how to read instruments and you have the feel for machinery. That takes ability, Roger. Ability and flair.'

'So there's a connection between –'

'Mylor and machinery? Yes, yes, indeed.'

'Mylor?' Angel challenged.

'That's the name of our horse,' Boff Parkway arrived grinning. Hopefully he was going to rub out the question marks. 'Mylor's a Celtic word meaning prince. He's royal all right – a prince among horses.'

'I can't wait to see him,' Angel enthused. 'Where do you stable him? Is it far? Can we go now?'

'We don't stable him,' Boff sounded offended. 'We–'

'Let's keep that a surprise,' the Professor interjected. 'Let Angel be our final test, Algernon.'

'Algernon?' Angel frowned.

'My grandson here.' The Professor patted Boff's tousled mop of black hair. 'Haven't you been introduced? Goodness, I'm forgetting my manners. Algernon, this is Angel Young–'

'Of course we've been introduced,' Boff blushed. 'It's just that ... well, it's just that I've never told my school friends my real name.'

'Al-ger-non.' Angel pronounced the three syllables slowly and giggled.

'You see what I mean?' Boff gritted his teeth.

'We call him Boff,' I said. 'It's short for boffin.'

'Why not Algy?' the Professor countered. 'That's short for Algernon.'

'Because he doesn't look like an Algy.'

'You think he looks like a boffin?'

Apart from his hair he looked like a scaled-down version of the Professor. Chubby face, steel-rimmed spectacles, high intelligent forehead. They could have been father and son. 'Very much so,' I said. 'He obviously takes after you.'

The Professor gave a slow, appreciative smile. 'He's certainly inherited my inventive talent. His plans for the new mazemobile show tremendous promise.'

'Is something wrong with the present one?' Angel queried.

'It's clapped out,' Boff said. 'Gramps made it the year I was born, so it must be twelve years old at least. Its guidance activators are on the blink and its verbal nursery rhyme starter is very old-fashioned. Didn't

16

you find it childish? I bet you did. I bet you were embarrassed reciting the ladybird poem.'

'No I wasn't.' A hint of redness ran over her small uptilted nose as she glanced quickly at me. 'I – I thought it was very clever.'

The Professor's quizzical, humorous grey eyes twinkled behind his spectacles. 'Then you'll be really impressed by my latest creation. It's the product of ten years' hard work.'

'Golly,' Angel caught her breath on a gasp. 'That's an incredibly long time.'

'It's an incredible invention, young lady, and I shall be watching your reaction to it very carefully.' He turned to Boff. 'Lead your friends to the workshop, Algernon.'

'Can we see Mylor first?' Angel's voice was laced with anticipation, but Boff just laughed as he motioned us towards a very large, windowless concrete building.

I could feel a vibration under my feet and hear a steady hum leaking from the walls. Spider could hear it too. He cuddled himself deep into Angel's arms, burying his face, not wishing to see what would soon be revealed.

The Professor indicated an illuminated button mounted to the side of an armoured steel door. 'This works from my thumbprint,' he said slowly. 'Only Algernon and I can gain entry by pushing it because only our prints have been computerised. Tomorrow we'll make sure the machine has a record of yours too.'

My thoughts raced as the metal shutter rattled and lifted. I just stood on the threshold and gaped. Workbenches cluttered with electronic equipment ran the length of the two side walls. The floor was paved in black and white stone, rather like a chessboard, with a knob-studded console standing on each corner square. Heavy-insulation cable snaked from chattering computers and coloured lights flashed intermittently as reams of punched tape ran from spool to spool.

Boff motioned to one of the consoles. He fiddled with the dials and a centre section of the floor slid effortlessly to one side. His hand hovered tentatively over a lever as he looked towards the Professor. 'All systems functioning normally, Gramps,' he advised. 'Ultra-violet wattage is at zero, power-storage regulator is registering enough energy for an indoor demonstration.'

'Is the hydroelectric permutator at green?'

'Green and locked on, Gramps.'

'Kinetic turbine normal?'

'Normal and steady. Gauge reads one over four.'

The Professor nodded and clamped his hands behind his back. His attire of tweed jacket, battered cord breeches and wellingtons seemed completely out of character in such a sophisticated workshop. 'Operate master-switch,' he ordered crisply.

Boff pulled the lever and the floor began to throb.

'You're about to meet my most ingenious creation,' the Professor announced, pulling a clay pipe from his pocket and lighting it attentively. 'Automation at its very best. Technology at its finest. Let me introduce –'

'*Mylor*,' Boff shouted dramatically, '*the most powerful horse in the world!*'

The floor came up slowly and the sight which greeted my eyes left me paralysed. It was all I could do to manage a soft whistle through my teeth. Angel's mouth fell open in amazement and even Spider popped his head up and looked stunned rather than frightened.

'C-crikey!' I stammered as the floor levelled.

'A magnificent animal, Roger,' the Professor beamed. 'Wouldn't you agree?'

He was more than magnificent, he was unbelievable. A ruggedly framed thoroughbred. A giant of a horse. Seventeen hands, at least, rich chestnut in colour with a white blaze and four white socks. His chest was massive, his eyes bold and arrogant, his ears large and pricked. The muscles running from the shoulders down to the forearm were colossal, as were his sturdy quarters. He just stood looking at us, swishing his tail casually, arching his beautiful neck.

Angel moved her mouth but no words came.

Boff grinned and said, 'Angel's speechless, Gramps. I think she's impressed.'

'Yes, indeed, my boy,' the Professor replied, puffing heartily on his pipe. 'Her mind is finding it difficult to comprehend that Mylor isn't real. It will take time for her to come to terms with the fact that such a life-like specimen is merely a machine.'

Angel walked forward as though in a trance. She stroked Mylor's soft velvety muzzle and he blew quietly down his nostrils and nuzzled her affectionately.

'Oh, Mylor, you're beautiful,' she smiled broadly. 'Are we going to be friends? I really think he likes me, Professor.'

'Of course he does, young lady. I've built into him numerous sensory circuits such as discernment and appreciation along with sight, hearing and touch. He also has an instinct circuit and it's that little piece of wire that's telling him you're a friend.'

'What powers him?' I asked, completely bemused. 'Does he have a special source of energy?'

'He relies on the sun,' Boff explained. 'His body is fitted with thousands of solar cells, so minute they're not visible to the naked eye.'

'In simplified terms,' the Professor put in, 'it's not unlike focusing the sun's rays with a magnifying glass. It produces radiant heat and this is turned into mechanical energy by Mylor's own solar generator. He hasn't had his quota of sunshine today, hence he's not very frisky. His zinc–air batteries are running a bit low.'

'Powered by sunshine,' I murmured, overwhelmed by it all. 'It's fantastic.'

'Yes, yes, indeed,' the Professor's bald head bobbed like a wind-up toy. 'All that untapped energy up there in the sky, staring us in the face, and it's free.'

Angel was inspecting Mylor very closely. She was running her hands over his supple silky skin, fingering his mane, scrutinising every inch of his muscular body. I saw a flicker in her eyes and knew what she was thinking. With her usual frankness she spoke out.

'If this isn't skin, then what is it?'

'A mixture of latex and thermoplastic resin moulded over a steel frame,' the Professor conceded. 'It has the texture of skin but it's much stronger and far more resilient. If Mylor gets a nick or a cut he doesn't bleed. He doesn't feel pain either. That's one circuit I've been careful to leave out.'

Angel's chin lifted, almost imperceptibly. 'You make it all sound so convincing,' she admitted, 'but I've grown up with horses. I help during weekends at our local riding school and I've won rosettes competing in gymkhanas. If this horse is a robot then I'd know it. I think he's real. I think the Professor is playing a very clever joke on us.'

'We hoped you'd say that.' Boff smiled expansively and strode towards Mylor. 'You were our final test so to speak. By thinking we've tricked you you've confirmed that he's perfect.'

'Yes, indeed.' The Professor looked relieved and

slightly jubilant. 'Thank you, Angel, for your expert opinion,' he said with a hint of apology in his voice. He brushed Mylor's forelock to one side and exposed a tiny red button. 'After the initial shock I think you'll be pleasantly surprised.'

The big horse was still nuzzling Angel, blowing gently down his nostrils, but he froze like a statue the instant the Professor's forefinger touched the button. 'Instinct circuits deactivated,' he told Boff. 'Mylor is now on manual.'

Boff crawled under the horse's chest and raised his hands, palms uppermost, to the ribcage. 'The slight join under here is the only giveaway,' he said, applying pressure.

There was the faintest of clicks as a door-shaped section of Mylor's underbelly swung open. It was hinged and supported by thin steel hawser which acted as hand-rails. As four treads were attached to the inside of the door it was easy to see how access could be gained to the machine's interior.

'Chest-hatch open, Gramps,' Boff confirmed. He turned to my sister. 'Well, Angel, do you still think it's a real horse?'

Angel had gone a little white. 'Zoot,' she said almost inaudibly.

Boff suppressed a grin. 'Take a look inside, Roger. Mylor's fully air-conditioned.'

I crept under the massive chest, stood on the bottom tread and gazed wondrously at the interior. It was like the cockpit of some futuristic aircraft. Up front, above all sorts of control gear and electronic apparatus, a video screen was beaming pictures of the Professor puffing merrily on his pipe. I guessed Mylor's eyes were miniature television cameras. I also understood now why the Professor had been concerned about my height. There was a column of three seats and very little room to manoeuvre. I reckoned we'd just about fit.

'Mylor can run faster and jump higher than any living horse.' Boff's voice filled the cockpit. I traced it to a speaker on the dash panel. I reasoned that Mylor's ears had been fitted with microphones capable of picking up all outside sound. 'He also has ten times the strength,' Boff continued. 'How do you feel about piloting such an animal?'

I was grinning like a Cheshire cat when I finally emerged. I didn't have to give an answer. My expression said it all and more.

Chapter Two

It took me a full week to master Mylor's intricate controls. Every morning and afternoon we would spend two four-hour sessions putting the horse through its paces. Angel would occupy the seat directly behind me, fulfilling her role as navigator and answering my numerous queries about how a real horse would react in such and such a situation. Boff sat at the rear, totally absorbed in the technical side, jotting down details of modifications and coping with any electronic problems that might arise. The ever-vigilant Professor would follow us across the acres of grassland in the mazemobile, constantly using a stop-watch and making unceasing calculations.

It was all tremendous fun and I was enjoying it immensely, but I knew the Professor hadn't spent ten years building Mylor just for fun and games. These practice sessions were taking us nearer to the real objective, to the final goal that would justify Mylor's existence. I'd asked Boff time and time again for an explanation but he'd always just grin and tell me to be patient. All would be revealed at the right time, he'd say. Telling me now might give me the jitters and upset the whole scheme.

His answers didn't make me feel any happier. This morning I was beginning to brood and this feeling of unrest was affecting my judgement. There was still an hour of trials left before lunch but I was in no mood to complete them. I flicked the scan-switch and waited for Mylor's eyes to locate the mazemobile. When it centred on the video screen I locked on the course, set the throttle at half-power, and pushed the pace-selector lever from canter to gallop. I didn't do it all that smoothly and the sudden thrust jerked us back in our seats.

'Hey, what's going on?' Boff nearly swallowed the pencil he'd been chewing.

'I want to talk with the Professor,' I said.

'But we haven't finished the trials. There's a malfunction in one of the stabilisers –'

'The stabiliser will have to wait – my talk won't.'

'Roger!' Angel's voice was sharp. 'What's got into you?'

The mazemobile was filling the video screen. A glance at the distance-indicator told me we were fifty yards from the vehicle and closing fast. I throttled back and eased the pace-selector into neutral. Mylor's hydraulics responded and his leg action slowed. At the ten yard marker I triggered the dead-stop mechanism and the horse dug in his heels. We skidded slightly on the soft turf and came to a halt.

'All systems at shut down,' I announced. 'Prepare to open chest-hatch.'

Angel unclipped her safety harness and leaned towards me. 'I repeat,' she said, breathing heavily against my neck. 'What on earth's got into you?'

'Are you unwell, Roger?' Boff looked concerned as he released the chest-hatch.

'I've never felt better,' I grunted. 'I'm just fed up with being kept in the dark.'

'Aren't you enjoying yourself?'

'Of course I am. It's just that … well it's just that now that I've mastered Mylor I'm itching to know how and when you plan to use him. I *am* the pilot. I should be told.'

Boff went to reply but the Professor beat him to it. 'Some sort of technical hitch?' he enquired, poking his head into the cockpit and squinting at us. 'You were doing so well too. It was most gratifying, yes indeed. At one point I clocked Mylor's speed at fifty-two miles an hour. That's the fastest time to date.'

The half-hearted way we greeted this news was enough to tell him something was wrong. As we climbed out he peered over his spectacle rims and fastened pensive eyes on Boff, waiting for an explanation.

'It's Roger, Gramps,' Boff said, 'he's getting impatient. I think perhaps it's time to outline the campaign.'

'Oh, dear.' The Professor's face dropped.

'Is it so terribly secret?' Angel was also getting inquisitive.

'Oh, dear,' the Professor said again. 'I suppose I should really tell you. I've been playing for time, hoping you'd get so attached to Mylor that it would be impossible for you to say no.'

'Say no to what?'

'Mylor is entered in a race,' Boff put in through an embarrassed little cough. 'It's quite a big race and it's vital that he should win, or at least beat the ... er ... other ... er ...'

'Special entries,' the Professor supplied.

'Yes,' Boff's face relaxed a little. 'The other special entries.'

'Special?' Angel frowned. 'In what way are they special?'

'Well they're ... er ... similar to Mylor.'

'Machines?'

He nodded. 'There are only five of them. The other runners are real live horses.'

He was beginning to fidget, rattling the coins in his pocket and tugging at the neck of his sweatshirt as if it was choking him. I had the feeling he was holding something back. 'You say it's quite a big race,' I probed. 'How big exactly?'

'Oo-er ... largish.'

'And does this race have a name?'

'Ye-es, the ... the Grand National.'

'*Grand National!*' My voice pitched high with astonishment. 'Have you lost your marbles!'

The Professor set his face solemnly. 'Don't you think Mylor's up to it?'

'Mylor might be, but I'm not. I can't steer him over fences that are –' I drew in a long breath. 'Well, you know how big they are.'

'They're certainly very large,' Angel provided.

'They're not large, Angel,' I said, 'they're flipping enormous.'

The Professor put a match to his pipe and sighed heavily. He mumbled something about dismantling the practice fences in the south field and added that there was always the chance he'd win the next ten-year competition – always supposing he lived that long.

Angel nudged me in the ribs and produced her pained, pleading expression. Boff lowered his eyes and scuffed his shoe sulkily against the turf. Even Spider peered out of the chest-hatch and whined. They were all doing their best to make me feel guilty and they were succeeding. 'Okay,' I said, raising both hands. 'You're trying to wear me down and you're making a good job of it. I'm not saying yes and I'm not saying no, but I've dozens of questions buzzing around my brain and they need answers.'

'Of course, Roger,' the Professor sympathised, producing cups and a thermos flask from the maze-mobile. 'Let us all have a tea break and relax for a while. Everything seems better over tea, yes indeed. Where would you like me to begin?'

'At the beginning?' I suggested.

'Excellent.' He patted the grass and Angel and I sat down. The sun was blazing in a cloudless blue sky so Boff set Mylor on solar-storage before joining us. I sipped at my tea and listened attentively to the Professor.

It took him fifteen minutes to unfold the story, and an absorbing one it was too. It centred around an organisation in Switzerland called the International Inventors' Institute – a sort of élite club for the finest brains in the world. Only one person was allowed to qualify for membership every ten years, so the Institute devised an almost impossible test for prospective candidates. Build a horse capable of winning the Grand National was this decade's task, and that ten-year period ended with this year's race. It was now or never.

'Gramps *must* win,' Boff pressed anxiously. 'You can't let him down, Roger, you just can't.'

I looked at the Professor. 'Did you say you've erected practice fences?'

'Exact replicas of those used in the National, including the water-jump.'

'Maybe it's possible...' I hesitated. 'How much time have we got?'

'A week. The race takes place next Saturday.'

I sucked in my breath. 'That's cutting it very fine.'

'We can do it.' Boff grinned boldly.

'It'll take a lot of practice and teamwork. I'll have to have a detailed plan of the course.'

'You'll get it. We'll leave nothing to chance.'

Angel's blue eyes were puzzled. 'These five other machines, Professor. Have you seen them?'

'That's against the Institute's rules, young lady. The scientists and inventors hoping to qualify for membership mustn't make contact with each other.

We won't know how good their horses are until the day.'

'They'll have to come close to perfection to fool the racecourse officials,' I remarked.

'Indeed, Roger. Yes, yes, indeed.'

'I suppose Mylor –' I broke off, shrugged.

'Is good enough?' the Professor supplied. 'Have you forgotten Angel's reaction the first time she saw him?'

'No, I haven't. But don't forget we'll be dealing with professionals; people with keen eyes who earn their living with horses.'

'You're worrying for nothing,' Boff smiled triumphantly as he glanced towards Mylor. 'He's flawless.'

I followed his gaze, letting my eyes wander over our four-legged companion; the gleaming chestnut coat highlighted by the sun, the rippling muscles, the fine mappings of veins in the powerful neck. Perhaps, if anything, he was a little too perfect. Or perhaps I was just looking for an excuse to duck out of the Professor's hare-brained scheme.

'You'll get your professional reaction, Roger,' the Professor leaned into the mazemobile and produced a saddle and bridle. 'Take Mylor out of Parkway to the Downs. You'll find training gallops there which are used by local racing stables. Mingle with the horses and their lads. It will be most enlightening, yes indeed.' He handed the tack to Angel. 'Do you feel up to it, young lady?'

She gulped. 'You want me to ride...'

'Well sit, rather than ride. Remember Roger will be at the controls. Just let Mylor's ears pick up your instructions and your brother can carry them out.'

'Zoot!' She perked up considerably.

I grimaced. 'And don't be bossy,' I said.

Boff got a foot on the first tread and stopped. 'Please remember, Angel, that the chest-hatch won't open when the saddle's on. With the girths attached we're trapped inside.'

She said she understood and began fastening the bridle. Boff and I climbed into Mylor and closed the chest-hatch behind us. I slipped into my position at the controls and snapped home the safety harness. Spider leapt out of the little box we'd built for him in the rear and took full advantage of the comfort offered by the free middle seat. As I switched on the video screen he cocked his head to one side, regarding the image curiously. Being stared at by a six-inch Professor Parkway wasn't all that easy for a dog to understand.

'What's the energy reading?' Boff threw a serious note into his voice.

'Two-thirds charged,' I said.

He glanced at his watch and jotted the time on his clipboard. 'Okay, switch off solar-storage, we've plenty of power for the trip.'

I obeyed the request, triggering Mylor's ear-mikes as I did so. Angel's voice filtered from the dash speaker:

'You'll have to give me a leg-up, Professor. He really is incredibly large.'

There was a jolt above our heads as she swung into the saddle. The mikes picked up the sound of stirrup-leathers being adjusted and feet waggling themselves into irons.

'Angel's aboard,' Boff announced. 'Slot in the maze-programmer. Switch all systems to stand-by.'

'All systems ready,' I confirmed.

The video beamed a picture of the Professor backing towards the mazemobile. He exchanged a quick word with Angel then thrust both thumbs in the air. 'All clear, Roger. Good luck.'

I pushed the pace-selector to trot and inched the

throttle forward. Angel gave a little gurgle of delight as Mylor got into his stride. We were on our way.

Swanfield racecourse was situated on the edge of the Downs. It had an open-plan perimeter training track which was eagerly used by the nearby racing stables. Several horse-boxes were parked under a dense overhang of trees and small groups of men in hacking jackets and jodhpurs were dotted around the boundary viewing the activity on the track through binoculars.

'Trainers, head lads and suchlike,' Boff gestured vaguely at the screen. 'Take Mylor closer, let them get a good look at him.'

Two racehorses, heavily sweat-flaked after completing a circuit of the course were jogged clear of the track by their riders. They were met by a smartly dressed man wielding a shooting-stick and a short, stocky, rather scruffily turned out individual with carroty hair which spiked out from beneath a flat cap. Typical racing men, I thought. I turned Mylor towards them and gently eased him into a canter.

'Well, whaddaya know?' Carrot-hair grinned showing tobacco-stained teeth as Mylor veered to a halt in front of him. 'If it ain't some little bird on a great big gee-gee.'

'Hello,' Angel said brightly. 'It's a lovely day for riding.'

'Yeah, s'pose it is,' Carrot-hair replied, screwing up his eyes and appearing far more interested in Mylor than the weather. He circled round the horse looking puzzled. Boff and I were glued to the video watching his every reaction. He removed his cap, scratched at his scalp and added, 'Nice lookin' 'orse you've got there, kid. Local is 'e? What-d'ye call 'im?'

'Don't be so inquisitive, Grogan,' the man with the

shooting-stick interposed. He turned to Angel and raised his trilby. 'I must apologise for my head lad's abruptness, my dear. He's sadly lacking in manners. I'm Major Palmer by the way. I own a training establishment just outside Swanfield.'

'Pleased to meet you, Major.' I felt the saddle move overhead as Angel leaned forward to shake hands. 'I'm Angel Young and I don't mind answering Mr Grogan's questions, honestly. My horse is called Mylor. He's trained privately – a few miles from here.'

'*Your* horse,' Grogan cut in. 'You own 'im?'

'Well, our horse really. There are several of us.'

'A syndicate, eh?'

'Y-yes,' Angel stammered a little, unsure of the word. 'Yes, that's right.'

'Well I'd say you've got yourselves a winner.' The Major turned to one of the riders, adding, 'What do you think of him, Paul?'

'Splendid physique, sir. I'd certainly like to get a leg either side of him.'

'Paul's a freelance National Hunt jockey,' the Major explained. 'One of the best. His opinion counts for a lot.'

'Thank you,' Angel said.

'My pleasure, miss.' His rugged, good-natured face creased into a smile. He shook his feet from the stirrups, swung a leg over his mount's withers and slid to the ground.

'What did I tell you, Roger,' Boff's voice broke into my thoughts. 'That guy's a jockey and even he's fooled. Mylor's perfect in every –'

'Jockey!' The word spilled out harshly. 'Have we got one?'

'G-got one?'

'To ride Mylor in the Grand National.'

31

'Oh, hell.'

I groaned internally. 'And you said you'd left nothing to chance.'

He moved his hands in a helpless gesture. 'I – I just forgot. I've had so much technical stuff to think about that some of the less important details –'

'Less important! A horse can't race without a jockey on his back.'

'I realise that,' he looked slightly sick. 'W-what do you suggest we do?'

I didn't have a simple answer. I turned my attention back to the video screen and the picture had changed. Major Palmer and the jockey called Paul were nowhere in sight. All I could see and hear was Grogan talking to the other rider, a stubborn-looking man with grizzled hair. I turned up the volume.

'I'd say this 'ere Mylor comes pretty close to resemblin' old Fireball. I'd say 'e could almost double for 'im. Are you thinkin' what I'm thinkin', Charlie?'

'Yeah,' the rider smiled unpleasantly. 'You've got a good point, Rusty. Apart from the four white socks there ain't a lot of difference.'

'The socks can be fixed,' Grogan growled. 'I'm int'rested in 'is speed.'

'Socks?' Angel sounded confused. 'Is there something special about them? I don't understand.'

'Nothin' for you to worry your pretty little head over. You've got a nice 'orse, kid. Is 'e as fast as 'e looks?'

'He's *very* fast. He's entered in the Grand National.'

'Is 'e now,' Grogan wiped the flat of his hand across his mouth. The fingers were short, yellowed by nicotine, with nails bitten almost to the quick. 'Did you 'ear that, Charlie? Mylor's running in the Grand ruddy National.'

'I don't believe it,' the rider mocked. 'He can't be *that* good.'

'He is that good,' Angel blurted out. 'He's the most powerful horse in the world!'

Grogan barked a laugh. 'The kid's got a sense of humour. Oh, that's funny, that's really very very funny.'

'I don't tell lies,' Angel said seriously.

'No, you just stretch the truth a little, eh?'

'Mylor's faster than any horse you've ever seen.'

'Then prove it,' the rider challenged. 'Deeds speak louder than words.'

'All right, I will.'

'You won't,' I murmured. I looked at Boff. 'They're trying to goad her into a speed test.'

He thought about that for a second, then said, 'I can't see the harm. It could be fun.'

'I don't trust them. What did this Grogan character mean when he said he could fix Mylor's socks? And who or what is Fireball?'

Angel was jabbing her heels into Mylor's flanks, clicking her tongue, and making noises of encouragement. When he didn't respond she sighed gustily and shouted, 'Oh, Roger, don't be such a pig!'

'Roger?' Grogan's eyes narrowed. 'I thought you said he was called Mylor?'

'H-he is. Roger's a sort of nickname – I sometimes call him that when he's ... well when he's stubborn.'

'Asleep, more like,' the rider sniffed. 'He ain't moved for the last five minutes.'

'Come on, Roger.' Boff was beginning to get anxious. 'You'll have to do something soon or they might get suspicious.'

'It's two miles round that circuit,' I pointed out.

'So what's two miles? The Grand National's four and a half.'

I clenched down hard on my teeth. I didn't know what to do for the best. It was a sarcastic remark from Grogan that finally helped make up my mind:

'Next time you come to the trainin' track, kid, bring your L-plates with you.'

'Right, that does it!' I gritted. I engaged the pace-selector and rammed the throttle forward. Mylor cut between them, the power hustling him into a scorching gallop. Grogan scattered from the screen and the sour-faced rider nearly lost his seat as his mount shied and whinnied protestingly.

'Take the speed up to fifty, Roger.' Angel's amplified voice burst from the speaker. 'Let's give our Mr Grogan a *real* demonstration.'

The curved ribbon of training track lay ahead. I took a firm grip on the steering, ran careful eyes over the gauges. I knew only too well that a slight error of judgement on my part and Angel could be in real trouble.

The speed-indicator needle hovered at thirty. I held it steady as we negotiated the first left-handed bend. There was no give in the ground and Mylor swung a trifle wide. The T-shaped steering grips shuddered beneath my fingers as for a fraction of a second his stride seemed to falter.

'That damn stabiliser,' Boff cursed. 'These left-handers are putting tremendous pressure on Mylor's right legs. You'll have to make allowances until I get the chance to strip it down.'

'Will it hold?' I asked, opening up the throttle as the track ahead straightened.

'He won't collapse, if that's what you mean. Just go easy on the bends.'

The needle climbed to forty. I held it there, waiting for the next left-handed curve to present itself on the video. When it did I throttled back to twenty and we took it without a trace of vibration.

'Faster!' Angel was saying. 'Am I riding a racehorse or a beach donkey?'

I glanced at Boff.

'Your sister's crazy,' he said, but his lips quirked into a smile as he added, 'Still, I suppose you've got to admire her spirit. Give it all you've got when we hit the home straight.'

We cruised steadily on the long uphill climb to the final bend. Mylor took the camber without so much as a murmur from the malfunctioning stabiliser and we turned smoothly into the demanding five-furlong run-in. Demanding, that is, is you're a living, breathing, flesh and blood thoroughbred. It was sometimes easy to forget that Mylor was none of these things. He didn't have to rely on ability and stamina to get him home. That was a responsibility governed by a fairly able pilot and a solar generator. I fisted the throttle wide, hearing the rhythm of hooves quicken as they pounded the turf beneath my seat. The speed-indicator needle leapt almost into the red sector of the gauge. We were clocking fifty-five miles an hour.

'Look at Grogan's face,' Boff pointed a finger at the right hand corner of the screen. 'There by the rails. I don't think he's leaning on them, I think they're propping him up.'

I grinned. 'Where's the rider – Charlie or whatever Grogan called him?'

'I can't see him. Everyone seems to have left, including the Major.'

Apart from one solitary horse-box the boundary did appear deserted. It had to be lunch time, I reasoned, stealing a glance at my watch. My stomach was starting to rumble, and I reckoned we ought to be making tracks for Parkway Grange. I eased Mylor into a canter, turned him towards Grogan and locked on. The distance-indicator ate up the yards. I engaged neutral and coasted to the rails.

The slightly open-mouthed face of the head lad filled the video. The dead-stop mechanism snatched us to a standstill.

'*Well*,' Angel said breathlessly, 'do you still think I tell lies?'

'S-sorry, kid,' Grogan's voice was shaky. 'I ain't never seen an 'orse that could run so fast. 'E's a marvel all right. Do you know 'e ain't even sweatin'?'

'Ain't 'e?' Angel's throat caught. 'I mean isn't he?'

'Pity Charlie couldn't 'ave seen 'im. Damn shame about poor Charlie's 'orse.'

'Why, what's happened?'

''E reared up against the rails as you left. Torn one of 'is forelegs quite bad. Charlie's taken 'im to the 'orse-box, to try and stop the bleeding.'

'Bleeding?' I felt the saddle shift over my head as Angel swung to the ground. 'Oh, that's really awful – and I'm partly responsible. Can I be of any help?'

'I dare say he could use you ... but I wouldn't go, miss. It ain't a pretty sight.'

'I'm not squeamish,' she announced almost desperately. 'Will you please hold Mylor while I take a look.'

'I don't think –'

'I insist!' I watched her push the reins into Grogan's hands and march smartly away.

Boff and I exchanged glances. 'She shouldn't have gone,' I said.

Boff chewed on his lip, offered no comment.

Grogan was stroking Mylor's muzzle and chuckling to himself. 'That's my beauty, Rusty will take care of you ... we're going into business, you and me ... we're gonna be rich...'

'I don't like the sound of this,' I gripped the pace-selector convulsively. 'I think we should –'

Grogan suddenly pulled something black and

36

floppy from the inside of his anorak. With a quick, efficient movement he threw it over Mylor's head and tucked it into the bridle. The video flickered and went blank.

'He's hooded Mylor!' Boff burst out. 'Hellfire, Roger, we're blind!'

My fingers felt damp against the pace-selector. I stared at the blacked-out screen, my mind groping feverishly for an answer to deal with the situation.

'Operate M-Mylor's instinct circuits,' Boff stammered. 'We can't help him now. It's up to him to help himself.'

I thumbed the switch to the 'instinct on' position and immediately our heads snapped back as Mylor reared. Boff managed to grab Spider's collar as the dog slid on all fours towards the tail-end. The horse seemed to be lashing out with his forelegs. The ear-mikes picked up several choice swear words as Grogan wrestled with the reins. Mylor pitched forward and although my body was anchored firmly by the safety harness, I couldn't prevent my elbow from crashing numbingly into the cockpit wall. I screwed up my face with the pain but I didn't cry out. Grogan had been joined by the rider called Charlie and their conversation sent an icy ripple of sweat down my backbone.

'What 'ave you done with the kid?'

'She's tied up in the cab. She won't give us any trouble.'

'Is the ramp down?'

'Yeah, it's down.'

'Then throw that halter around this crazy animal's neck and 'elp me get 'im to the box.'

There was a slap and a jerk as the halter made contact. Mylor shook his head furiously in an attempt to get free but the odds were stacked against him. He

Grogan threw something black and floppy over Mylor's head and tucked it into the bridle. 'He's hooded Mylor!' Boff burst out. 'Hellfire, Roger, we're blind!'

was fighting anger and confusion and he was losing. With the hood attached he was blind and powerless. He was totally disorientated and there was no other choice but to surrender. In an obvious state of distress he walked slowly forward.

'We're entering the horse-box,' Boff said as hooves rattled metallically on the ramp.

I swallowed hard, listening as the halter was fastened. There was the shuffle of feet, a few indistinct murmurs of speech, and then the long groan of oil-starved hinges as the ramp slammed shut.

It was growing hot inside Mylor and my thoughts were fogging. I unclipped my safety harness and stripped off my shirt. I felt my pulse speed up as my fingers worked anxiously at the chest-hatch release lever. I waggled it to and fro but the door wouldn't budge. I remembered the saddle and girths and slammed my fist against my thigh in frustration.

'Save your energy, Roger,' Boff said. 'They won't remove the tack until they reach their destination.'

'Can't we do anything?'

'Only sit and wait. I'm afraid Mylor wasn't designed to cope with...' He broke off with an exasperated shrug.

The barely audible rumble of an engine echoed from the dash speaker. There was a grating of gears and a shudder from the rear wheels as the transmission took up the strain. The horse-box was on the move.

I made my way despondently back to my seat. The ear-mikes were picking up the sound of a scream. Angel's scream. A noise that was instantly turned into a gurgle, as if someone had clamped a hand over her mouth. Anger boiled inside me. My mind was full of images of Grogan manhandling her.

'Damn those girths!' I growled, smothering the speaker-grille with my palm.

Chapter Three

Time passed and a very frustrating time it was too. We were cooped up in that horse-box for what seemed like an eternity. The journey had only lasted ten minutes but we'd been parked now for several hours without anybody making an attempt to come near us.

Mylor was getting restless. He didn't like being hooded and his instinct circuits were constantly fighting the halter. His head swung like a seesaw, rasping the leather strap against its securing ring. Boff and I just sat looking at each other, listening to the pendular rhythm tick the seconds away. Spider had decided that the middle seat wasn't such a good idea after all and was now curled up in his little box at the rear.

'Three thirty,' I said, eyeing my watch for what must have been the hundredth time. 'You should have tackled the faulty stabiliser, Boff, at least that would have kept you occupied.'

'I was just thinking the same thing,' he admitted sombrely. 'I could have had it fixed and put back together by now.' He heaved a sigh and added, 'How was I to know they'd keep us here for this long? I might have started, they might have come, and then Mylor would have limped out on three legs.'

I nodded and went to rest my chin on my hands. The ramp groaned and cancelled the movement. Boff and I leaned anxiously towards the dash speaker.

'I thought the Major weren't never gonna leave,' Grogan was saying 'We ain't gotta lot of time, Charlie, so keep your eyes peeled. You bring that broken-winded old nag in 'ere while I take Mylor to the loose-box.'

There was a whinny and the shuffle of steel shoes on the ramp. The ear-mikes were picking up Grogan's muttered curses and the loud rustle of cloth. The video suddenly flickered and brightened. Cold, amber eyes seemed to be studying us critically. A cigarette waggled between thick lips as Grogan announced, 'The hood ain't done 'im no 'arm. If anythin' it's calmed the headstrong basket down.'

He moved away and began to untie the halter. As the pressure slackened, Mylor swung his head to the left and for a moment I thought we were looking at his reflection in a mirror.

'Grief!' Boff's lips tightened. 'I-It's another horse. A d-double.'

Certainly at first glance they did appear identical. Same colouring, same white blaze; the head came close to being a carbon copy. It was only as Grogan turned Mylor to lead him down the ramp that the main difference became apparent. Apart from the obvious lack of muscle, this horse had only two white socks whereas Mylor had four.

I pulled my thoughts together with an effort. 'It's a switch,' I said. 'They're exchanging Mylor for –'

'Fireball.' Boff indicated the video. We were being led towards a loose-box which bore the nameplate.

I swallowed hard, watching the screen.

'We could always put Mylor on manual,' Boff suggested. 'Power our way out.'

'And leave Angel behind?'

'Oh,' he pulled his ear gently, 'perhaps that's not such a good idea.'

'We all leave together, Boff, or we don't leave at all.'

41

He gave his ear a final tug. 'Then I guess we sit tight.'

Grogan had been joined by a stringy-looking youth with hollow cheeks and a sallow complexion. His sweater had more holes in it than a Gruyère cheese, his jeans were patched, and his shoes worn down at the heels.

'Move yourself, Ought!' Grogan snapped. 'Get Fireball's tack off and give 'im some oatmeal gruel. 'E's had an 'ard work-out on the Downs.'

'I didn't even know he'd gone,' the youth said, scratching his neck absently. 'Is that one of our saddles? It looks brand new t'me.'

'That's because it *is* brand new. It's mine, Ought. I saved for it out of me wages. Now get it off and use those skinny little 'ands of yours to wash off the grease and rub in the saddle soap.'

I heard the sweat flap being lifted and the faint tinkle of buckles as someone tugged at the girth leathers.

'Why does Grogan keep calling him Ought?' Boff asked, puzzled. 'Is that a surname or what?'

I shrugged. I wasn't particularly interested. The girths were hanging loose, the saddle was shifting overhead, and that meant freedom.

'Something's different about this horse,' Ought was saying. 'He's got bigger and ... hey, Rusty, what's happened to his hindlegs?'

''Appened?'

'The white markings. He's got four socks instead of two.'

'Now ain't you observant,' Grogan's mouth twitched unpleasantly. He took a long pull on his cigarette, letting a stream of smoke trickle from his nostrils. He leant against the manger, adding, 'Come 'ere, my half-starved little friend. Rusty Grogan thinks it's time you and 'im 'ad a chat.'

'W-what?'

'Come 'ere – now!'

Boff's eyes were suddenly huge behind the lenses of his spectacles. They stared unblinkingly at the video, watching as Grogan removed the cigarette from his lips and blew gently on the glowing end. Ought edged his way gingerly into our picture and stopped about a yard short of the head lad.

Grogan said lazily, 'You're thinkin' nasty thoughts. Tell Rusty about 'em.'

'N-no I'm not. I'm –'

Grogan grabbed him around the throat and pinned him against the manger. 'I wanna know what's going on in Ought's head,' he snarled, pulling up a sleeve of the boy's ravelled sweater and holding the tip of the cigarette dangerously near to the skin. 'I think Ought better tell me before I stub this out on 'is wrist.'

'Please, Rusty...'

'I'm waiting,' the cigarette wobbled as Grogan sniggered. 'Tell me about Fireball.'

'I – I don't think it is Fireball.'

'You're thinking well. Tell me more,'

'F-Fireball runs at Chepstow on Monday ... Charlie Carver rides him.'

'So?'

'Carver's a fiddler. I reckon you're both planning to bet heavily on Fireball's substitute and win yourselves a packet of money.'

'Right in one.' Grogan's quick, temperamental eyes flashed. 'And what is Ought gonna do about this? Tell the Major or keep 'is trap shut?'

'I won't say anything. I ... I promise.'

'Good boy,' Grogan smiled with swaggering self-confidence as he pinched out the cigarette and dropped the unsmoked half into the pocket of his anorak.

43

'Now you go and prepare 'is gruel while I mix up the brown stain for 'is feet.'

As Grogan drew back the bolt on the loose-box door Mylor swung viciously towards him. He drove his muzzle hard into the head lad's neck and sent him sprawling into the cobbled yard. The ear-mikes picked up a thump and a groan, and a flat cap went spinning across the video screen.

'Instinct circuits functioning normally,' Boff remarked through a grin. 'I don't think Mylor's all that fond of our Mr Grogan.'

Ought was thinking the same thing. He held Angel's saddle up to his eyes in an effort to keep a straight face but his shoulders were shaking with laughter. 'The horse must have heard you, Rusty,' he blurted. 'Something tells me he's not going to like having his feet dyed.'

'None of your lip!' Grogan emerged looking a little dirtier than before. He massaged his neck then took time off to deliver a hefty kick to Ought's backside. The boy let out a yelp and limped away. Grogan slammed the bottom half of the box door shut and thrust a warning finger at Mylor. 'Don't get skittish with me or I'll flay your hide!' he threatened, before slouching off.

'You'd only find bare metal if you did,' Boff muttered, watching the figure diminish on the video.

'Shall I shut down all systems?' I asked.

He nodded. 'We'll operate the forelock button once we're out. What's the energy reading?'

'Just under a third charged.'

'Hell's teeth!'

'We used a lot of power on that two-mile gallop,' I pointed out. 'Have we enough left to get back to Parkway Grange?'

He wagged his head doubtfully. 'Not without a recharge we haven't. Switch on the solar-storage, Roger. Somehow we've got to get Mylor out of this box and into the sun.'

There was a slight hiss from the pneumatic dampener as Boff released the chest-hatch. We climbed stealthily down the treads to the straw. It felt good just being able to stand upright and stretch our limbs. I pulled Spider's leash from my pocket and coaxed him out of his box. I reckoned we would have to make full use of that little sniffer if we were to stand any chance of finding Angel reasonably quickly.

We tossed a coin for who should do what. Boff won and he plumped for the job of looking for my sister. With Spider at his heels he made a casual exit from the box and strolled nonchalantly across the yard. Nobody stopped him and the place seemed deserted. Being Saturday afternoon, I reasoned, most of the stable staff had probably gone to the races. I closed the chest-hatch and put Mylor's instinct circuits back into operation by depressing the forelock button. I could see some horses grazing in a distant paddock and I had the idea that if I could get Mylor across to them – lose him amongst them – then hopefully he would go unnoticed and his solar cells could gather what little sunshine the day still offered.

His moist, trusting eyes swung towards me as I took hold of his flaxen mane. There was an invisible bond between us, a deep affection which had been growing steadily since the day we'd first met. He was so perfect, his characteristics so human, that I was finding it increasingly difficult to think of him as a machine. 'Atta boy, Mylor,' I breathed, leading him gently out of the box. 'You'll soon perk up when you feel the sun –'

'Hey! Where do you think you're going with that horse!'

There was a slight hiss from the pneumatic dampener as Boff released the chest-hatch. He climbed stealthily down the treads to the straw.

The exclamation stopped me dead in my tracks, but Mylor took an extra stride forward and his chest clipped the plastic bucket in Ought's outstretched hand. The boy winced as steaming gruel slopped like lava over his jeans and shoes.

'Now look what you've – I'm soaked! What are you doing here? Who are you?'

I met his gaze levelly. 'I've come to collect my horse. My name's Roger Young.'

'*Your* horse?' He sounded sceptical.

'I'm one of a syndicate,' I announced, remembering Grogan's word, 'and I ... er ... we don't care much for horse thieves.'

He rubbed his knuckles against his teeth. 'I'm no horse thief. I have to work here so I follow the head lad's instructions.'

'Are you a jockey?'

'Heck, no. I'm just a stable lad.'

'Oh.'

He must have seen my face drop because he asked, 'Are you looking for a jockey?'

'We need one rather badly.' I patted Mylor's softly ridged neck muscles. 'Our horse – this horse – runs in the Grand National.'

'Blimey, then you need the best. I suppose I ought to recommend Charlie Carver or Ray –'

'What about Paul?' I suggested, remembering how highly the Major had praised him.

'Paul Steel?'

'Is he about twenty-five, well tanned, with dark wavy hair?'

'Yes he is, but he's freelance and always fully booked. Have you met him?'

'He was at Swanfield's training track just before Grogan snatched our horse.'

'Don't remind me about Grogan,' he muttered.

47

'And don't hang around here where he can see you.'
He clicked his tongue and backed Mylor into the box.
'If Grogan finds you with me you'll get done for sure.'

'I'm not scared of Grogan,' I stated, trying to sound
far more fearless than I felt. 'I'm going to report him
to Major Palmer—'

'Are you crazy? He eats little boys like you for
breakfast. Take a look at these.' He dragged back his
sleeve and showed me half a dozen tiny white circular
scars. 'Grogan gets his kicks out of burning people.
You do as you're told or you get hurt. There isn't a
lad in the yard who'll stand up to him.'

'So why doesn't somebody tell the Major?'

'Because Rusty Grogan's too good at pulling the
wool over the Major's eyes. He's thirty-eight and the
head lad – and that counts for a lot. I'm sixteen, right.
If I complain, who do you think the Major is going to
believe?' He shook his head slowly, slackly. 'No, mate,
I say nothing because I want to keep my job.'

I sucked in my breath impatiently. 'Does that mean
you aren't going to help me?'

He scratched his jaw, mentally weighing me up.
'How'd you get here anyway?'

'There isn't only me, there are three of us and a
dog.'

'All right, so how did three of you and a dog get
here?'

'Grogan forced my sister against her will. The rest
of us ... well we ...'

'Yes?'

I made a few unintelligible noises, swallowed hard,
and decided to change the subject. 'This horse must
have some sunshine,' I croaked.

'Eh?'

'Sunshine,' I repeated. 'Can you put him in the
paddock for an hour?'

'Are you crazy?' His eyes wandered from me to the empty bucket. 'This horse doesn't need exercise, he needs nourishment. Because of your blasted clumsiness, I've got to mix up some more oatmeal gruel.'

'I wouldn't bother. He doesn't eat oatmeal gruel.'

'So what does he eat?'

'He doesn't.'

'Doesn't?'

'Eat.'

'You *are* crazy, do you know that? Blooming crackers, that's what.'

'He's a very special horse,' I said lamely.

He managed a tight smile. 'He isn't only special, Master Roger loony Young, he's darned well unique.' He stabbed a finger in my chest and added, 'I ought to report you for trespassing. I ought to hand you over to Grogan. Heck, there's a hundred and one things I ought to do.'

'Then why don't you?'

'Because I've never been very good at making decisions.'

I was beginning to understand how he'd obtained his nickname. 'But you do believe I own the horse?'

He pondered the question. With a wriggle of his bony shoulders he said, 'Well I know it isn't Fireball. I suppose somebody must own –' His voice trailed off. The sound of approaching footsteps caused moisture to stand out on the taut skin below his hairline. 'Grogan,' he whispered.

'What shall I do?' I asked numbly.

'I suppose you ought to hide.'

I glanced at Mylor, contemplating the chest-hatch. It was the obvious place but I couldn't risk it in front of Ought. The footsteps were coming from the right and luckily the bottom half of the door was hinged on the right and open. I crouched down, used the door as a shield, and scurried to the loose-box on my left. I freed the two securing bolts without much difficulty and wriggled my way inside. A scrawny-looking grey colt regarded me curiously, fluttered his nostrils, and backed away.

'What's this mess?' Grogan was saying, jabbing at the tarmac with his boot. 'You've spilt the gruel, 'aven't you? You've slopped it all over the ground instead of putting it in the ruddy manger.'

'I – I only lost a little, Rusty.'

'The hell you did! 'Ave you seen the state of your shoes? I'm gonna teach you a lesson you won't forget in an 'urry –'

'Ugh – ah – *achh*!' There was a strained retching noise followed by a loud thump which shook the adjoining wall.

'Jus' keep outa my way – get it!'

'I – I've got it.' Ought's voice sounded close to tears.

'Do you think you can 'old this 'orse steady while I apply the dye?' Grogan mocked. 'Or do you think you oughta be doing somethin' else? There must be lots of oughts you should've done but ain't.'

'I suppose I ought to have cleaned your saddle by now.'

'Yes, you *ought*!' There was the slap of fingers landing on flesh. 'You're gonna be workin' late, ain't you? Now get a grip on this 'orse!'

I stalked the box, feeling my fists tighten, my heart begin to pound. The thought of Grogan messing around with Mylor's feet made my blood run cold. He'd have to squat low to apply the dye and that ran the risk of him spotting the chest-hatch join. Also, all the time Mylor remained on instinct he was using power. Deprived of sun, his special zinc-air batteries would get lower and lower and he would grow progressively weaker.

The rasp of boots on the tarmac outside interrupted my thoughts. I ducked back into the shadows on catching a glance of Charlie Carver's hard face with that almost lipless mouth and bony chin. He lurched into Fireball's box and exchanged muffled words with Grogan. Ought made an exit a few seconds later and limped across the yard swinging the plastic bucket, his footsteps drowned by Grogan's persistent requests for a fresh supply of oatmeal gruel. As I watched him disappear, something flickered in the corner of my vision. Boff and Spider were emerging from the other direction. I beckoned frantically to them.

'We've found Ang –' Boff began, stopping mid-sentence as I pressed a finger to my lips.

'Not so loud,' I breathed. 'Grogan's next door.'

'Sorry,' he lowered his voice, 'but I thought you'd like to know that Spider's managed to sniff out your sister. She's in an old building round the back with three horseshoes nailed to the door. I couldn't let her out because the door's fitted with a very high bolt. There wasn't any way I could reach it.'

'Do you know if she's okay?'

'I think she's bound and gagged, but I could hear some movement – as if she was struggling to get free.'

I nodded, relieved. My mind began turning over various ways of tackling the high bolt. I reckoned we could always wheedle it free with a broom handle, or else Boff could sit on my shoulders and loosen it by hand. The second idea seemed the more positive and I was about to suggest it when a loud remark from Grogan pulled me up short.

'I ain't never seen an 'orse with skin like this!' he complained. 'The dye's simply runnin' off, Charlie. It's like trying to paint greaseproof paper with a kid's box of water-colours.'

'Kinda weird,' Carver agreed. 'is it good quality dye?'

'The best. Get it on your 'ands and it'll take a week of 'ard scrubbin' to get it off.'

'Well it ain't staying on those socks, that's for sure.'

'Feel 'em, Charlie,' Grogan suggested. 'Feel the texture of the hair. Don't it strike you as odd?'

'Yeah, it's sorta rubbery. Perhaps the girl's been grooming him with some new product.'

Boff smirked. 'Latex and thermoplastic resin, eh, Roger? And you can't stain that with a conventional dye.' He dipped into his pocket, pulled out a sausage roll, and bit into it. 'Hard cheese, Mr Grogan. You're just wasting your time.'

My mouth fell open. 'Where did you get...?'

'Oh, the Professor experimented with various chemical—'

'No, not the latex and the thermoplastic whatnot — the sausage roll.'

'The stable-lads' kitchen,' he said, wiping crumbs of flaky pastry from his lips. 'There was nobody about and there was this whole pile — say, do you want one?'

'I'm starving.'

'Then help yourself. I've a whole pocketful ... *Eeek*!' The grey colt's muzzle had sniffed out the fact and Boff overbalanced as he took an involuntary step backwards. His shoulders hit the box door with a crack but I managed to stifle a second yell by cramming my hand over his mouth.

'Sssh!' I whispered very firmly against his ear.

'I can't ... breathe,' he protested.

The colt's mane brushed my arm and chest as he foraged in Boff's pocket. Sausage rolls were tumbling all over the place and Spider was having a great time chasing them around the straw until they broke up into small enough pieces for him to swallow.

'Smokey Joe's getting a bit restless.' Grogan's voice floated towards us. 'Better take a look, Charlie – see what's botherin' 'im.'

Carver said, 'He's impatient for his five o'clock feed, that's all.'

'I thought I 'eard a voice.'

Boff looked at me, licked his lips. I could feel my stomach tightening.

'Whoa!' Grogan shouted the command. There was a clatter as Mylor's hooves hit the water bucket and a gasp of protest from Carver as the horse lunged forward. The box door shook violently and there was a rending creak as wood splintered under the strain.

'Holy Moses!' Carver's voice was shrill. 'He's burst the top bolt, Rusty. He's got so much power –'

'And we're gonna make full use of that power when you ride 'im on Monday,' Grogan broke in. 'The bookmakers will think 'e's Fireball, right? We should be able to get odds of 20–1 at least. I'll back 'im with the 'undred quid we've got stashed away and that should win us...' he paused, sniggered quietly, 'two luverly grand.'

Boff was doing mental calculations. 'That's two thousand pounds,' he said.

I hardly heard him. I was letting my breath out slowly, grateful to Mylor for creating the rumpus and distracting their attention away from us.

The distant throb of an engine heralded someone's arrival. Grogan heard it too. He was beginning to panic and a lot of disjointed sentences were coming our way.

'That sounds like the Major ... Get rid of the dye ... What the hell's he doing back so early...'

Charlie Carver made a hurried exit from the box and just managed to scoot across the cobbles before a cream Range-Rover rumbled into the yard. It screeched to a halt in front of the office and Major Palmer and Paul Steel climbed out.

'Let's go, Boff.' I tucked Spider under my arm and slipped the bolts. 'Rusty Grogan's going to have an awful lot of explaining to do.'

The Major frowned slightly as we marched towards him. He exchanged glances with Paul who just folded his arms and regarded us levelly. I turned to look back at Mylor and my eyes locked briefly with Grogan's. His face went a little chalky before he ducked back into the shadow of the box.

'If you're looking for weekend work –' the Major began.

'We're not, sir,' I said. 'We've come to collect our horse.'

'Horse?'

'Mylor.'

'Haven't got an animal here of that name,' the Major was adamant. 'You've obviously got the wrong yard.'

'The name seems familiar though,' Paul rubbed his sunburned jaw thoughtfully. 'I've got it. He's a big handsome fellow – a chestnut – ridden by a girl with blonde hair.' He hesitated, then snapped his fingers. 'Angel somebody or other.'

'Young,' I supplied.

'Looked about twelve to me,' the Major swivelled his gaze to Boff. 'I remember her now. Spoke to her at the training track. I was full of misgivings. She seemed far too young to be riding such a strong –'

'You don't understand, sir,' Boff cut him off. 'Her surname is Young and this is her brother, Roger.'

The Major fingered the brim of his trilby and looked confused. 'Well, now I've met them both. Brother *and* sister. I'm afraid I still don't see –'

'Angel and Mylor are here,' I interjected. 'They're

being held prisoner.'

The statement jolted him. He leaned against the Range-Rover and gave me the kind of look which demanded answers. I told him in detail everything that had happened. Well, not entirely in detail – I left out things like ear-mikes and video screens and the journey from the training track to the stables in the horse box. I covered by telling him we'd been hiding in some nearby bushes when Grogan and Carver had snatched Mylor, and that the name painted on the side of the horse box had led us to the stables.

My story caused a little nerve to flutter on the side of his face. It eventually lost itself in his wrinkles and he said dubiously, 'Well either you've got a vivid imagination, young man, or I've got a thoroughly untrustworthy head lad.'

'I've never liked Rusty Grogan,' Paul sided with us, clapping a hand on my shoulder. He turned to the Major. 'I suggest we see for ourselves. Let's take a long hard look at the horse in Fireball's box.'

Grogan's eyes watched us approach from beneath flat, sweaty lids. I could hear his heavy breathing and he was mumbling to himself. He'd managed to lay his hands on a body brush and curry comb and was making a pretence of vigorously grooming Mylor.

'Aft'noon, Major, sir,' he touched his cap, formed his lips into a smile. 'You and Paul are back early – nothin' wrong I 'ope?'

'Paul's lost his Grand National ride,' Major Palmer said stonily. 'His mount's gone lame, sprained a hock by the look of it.'

'That's most distressin', sir. Let me offer my –'

'Fireball's looking healthy,' Paul interrupted, tapping his white teeth with a fingernail. 'Been using a lot of elbow grease, Rusty?'

Grogan smiled again but there wasn't anything humorous about it. 'You can't be lookin' very 'ard, Paul,' he said. 'This 'orse 'as four white socks whereas Fireball's only got two.'

'You were going to dye them!' Boff burst in. 'You were going to use our horse to win yourself two thousand pounds!'

'Me?' Grogan's expression of astonishment would have put an actor to shame. 'You do someone a good turn and you get accused...' He broke off, sighed. 'I wish now I'd left the poor 'orse running loose on the trainin' track. I spent 'alf an hour lookin' for the little girl too. There ain't no justice.'

The Major rubbed a lean hand over his eyes. 'I think you'd better explain, Grogan,' he said.

Boff and I listened, astounded, as the lies just poured from his mouth. In his version he'd cast Carver and himself as heroes. They'd spent quite a time trying to catch Mylor who was roaming loose and frightened, and as they couldn't find a trace of the girl who'd been riding him they'd decided to bring him back to the stables for safety. Fireball's box happened to be the most convenient because Fireball was being transported to the farrier for re-shoeing.

' 'Spect some other stable found the girl,' he added, watching me closely. 'Charlie and I looked everywhere but we couldn't find 'er.'

Paul's gaze travelled to the splintered wood and broken bolt. 'How did this happen?' he asked.

'Mylor done it. This 'orse don't know his own strength – he jus' pounded into the door.'

'He's not marked.'

'He's a tough'n all right. I reckon he thinks he's made of metal.'

Boff coughed, swallowed hard. 'W-we want to take him home. We know you've got Angel here so don't pretend otherwise.'

Grogan's eyes narrowed into slits. 'I don't think I like your tone, sonny. Are you callin' me a liar?'

Boff shrank back under the head lad's hostile glare.

Paul leaned forward, the muscles tightening along his solid jaw. 'I believe these kids,' he said thickly. 'So I guess *I'm* calling you a liar.'

'Now look, Mr Steel—'

'No, you look, Mr Grogan. Where's the girl!'

'Locked behind a door with three horseshoes nailed to it,' Boff went on quickly. 'Spider traced the scent — I know she's there.'

'That's the racing tack-room,' Major Palmer remarked.

Grogan's knuckles whitened on the body brush. 'She ... she ain't there ... I swear it. You've gotta believe me, Major. These kids 'ave been readin' too many comics.'

'Prove it,' Paul challenged, grabbing a lapel of Grogan's anorak and yanking him out of the box. 'Lead the way and show us how wrong we are.'

He made a few noises of protest but Paul's strong fingers just took a firmer hold and dragged him into the yard. We set a determined course for the racing tack-room.

'I only hope you're right,' I whispered to Boff as we reached the door with the three horseshoes.

'Of course I'm right.' He indicated Spider who was making little whimpering noises and scraping his front paws frantically against the woodwork.

'Open it, Grogan,' the Major ordered crisply.

Sweat beaded his forehead. He cuffed it away and lifted trembling fingers towards the high bolt. It slipped free of its keeper and the hinges squealed as the door swung towards us.

No Angel. Just the smell of liniment and the sight

of saddle cloths and well oiled leather. My heart sank. Spider ran in to examine all the nooks and crannies but they revealed only emptiness.

Grogan wasn't sweating any more. He seemed both relieved and surprised. He shook himself free of Paul's grip and said scornfully, 'I think you've gone soft in the head. Fancy believin' a couple of screwy kids.'

Chapter Four

Paul secured Mylor with a head collar and led him from Fireball's box. All of us were looking glum and none of us felt like talking very much. I had this inner feeling that something terrible had happened to Angel. I felt it in the pit of my stomach, knowing I was helpless, knowing that there was nothing left for us to do but return to Parkway Grange.

'She'll turn up, Roger,' Paul made an effort to cheer me. 'Who knows, she might even be waiting for you when you get back.'

I shook my head listlessly. 'She's here,' I said. 'I know it but there's no way I can prove it.'

'She was definitely in that tack-room.' Boff removed his glasses and squinted at me as he polished the lenses. 'Somebody must have moved her, that's the only logical answer.'

'Well it couldn't have been Grogan.'

'Perhaps Charlie Carver . . .?'

'Not enough time.'

Paul hesitated. 'Have either of you considered the possibility that Angel might have freed herself? That's a very old bolt and if it wasn't properly locked it wouldn't take too much kicking to jiggle it free.'

'That's true,' Boff agreed.

My gaze fell miserably to my clenched hands. 'It was properly locked when we arrived,' I murmured. 'If she'd escaped in the way Paul suggests she wouldn't have refastened the bolt. She's far too short.'

'I guess not,' Paul admitted, 'so after I've taken you home I'll come back here and give the place a thorough search.'

'*You're* taking us home?'

He indicated a Rice trailer. 'I'll hitch that to the Range-Rover and have you back at Parkway Grange within minutes. Don't tell me you'd prefer to ride?'

'We couldn't anyway because Mylor's energy level—' Boff pulled himself up short. 'Er ... what I mean is we're all very tired and...' He faltered again, scratched his neck and smiled thinly. 'Th-thanks, Paul, a lift would be very welcome.'

'That's what I thought.' The jockey looked faintly surprised.

Grogan was watching our activity with interest. He stood coiled in the office doorway, smoking heavily, his eyes flitting from us to Paul as the trailer was coupled to the Range-Rover.

'I'm sure he was as surprised as we were at not finding Angel in the tack-room,' Boff submitted. 'Look at the expression on his face. He's baffled, Roger. Baffled and confused.'

'Grogan's a crook,' I grunted sourly.

'And Carver?'

'They're both crooks.'

'Lucky we've found a friend.' Boff thrust his chin towards Paul.

I nodded, watching the jockey's lean brown hands expertly reverse the Range-Rover and trailer to within a few feet of us He notched on the handbrake and showed us that big white reassuring smile of his.

'This isn't a good moment to suggest this, Roger,' Boff began hesitantly, 'but as Paul's lost his Grand National ride I think we should—'

'Ask him if he'd like to ride Mylor?'

'Well ... yes. I know it's very selfish to be thinking of the race at a time when Angel's missing—'

'Go ahead.'

'Y-you don't mind?'

'I feel tired, hungry, depressed and not very sure about anything any more – but I do know you'd be stupid if you passed up the opportunity of getting a first-class jockey for Mylor.'

'Wow, thanks, Roger.' His expression was eager. 'I'll ask him now.'

Paul Steel came towards us, thumbs loosely hooked in the waistband of his jodhpurs. His deep grey eyes gave the impression of firmness and self-confidence. I knew he was the man for Mylor. I knew that with him on our back we could win. It was only the uncertainty about Angel that stopped my enthusiasm from showing on my face.

'I – I have a proposition for you, Paul,' Boff cleared his throat and began a little shakily. 'Our horse is entered in the Grand National and I wondered ... er ... if you would consider...'

'We'd like to engage you to ride him,' I explained quickly on seeing the jockey's forehead begin to crease into a frown.

'You want me...?'

'We'd be very grateful.'

He rubbed his jaw, ran his eyes carefully over Mylor. 'But I don't know anything about your horse, boys. He looks big and strong and fit – but how fast is he? Can he tackle fences as high as those in the National?'

'He can tackle fences twice as high,' Boff said sharply. 'He's the most powerful horse in the world.'

Paul's eyes lit with a gleam of amusement. He reached into the pocket of his denim shirt, produced a lump of sugar and offered it to Mylor. 'That's some reputation you've got, fella,' he grinned. 'Have a piece of this to keep up your stamina.'

Mylor's muzzle twitched as he felt the warmth of

Paul's hand. He had circuits to cope with smell and touch but things like taste didn't count. A sugar cube to Mylor was like a newspaper to a blind man. It could have no useful purpose and therefore it was ignored.

'I don't believe it,' Paul's eyes expressed surprise. 'I've never known a horse refuse –'

The sudden rasp of a Klaxon horn speared the air. I lost my balance as Mylor took a few uneven steps backwards. His ears flattened and his nostrils flared as the strangest and most colourful horse-box I'd ever seen in my life rattled and banged its way into the yard. It looked more like a fairground vehicle with its bright psychedelic paintwork, huge whitewall tyres and glitter lettering which spanned from the cab to the rear number-plate. It proclaimed: *Doctor von Sternberg*.

I managed to regain my grip on Mylor's head collar and stop him from backing up. I wasn't helped by von Sternberg's radiator which hissed and gurgled and belched out steam. Mylor swished his tail and restlessly shook his neck. He calmed slightly as the horse-box shuddered to a halt and the chattering old engine was switched off.

'Who on earth ...?' whispered Boff, awe-struck.

The cab door was thrown open and a dapper little man clutching a black doctor's bag leapt out to greet us. A Tyrolean hat with a feather in the side was perched rakishly on his head and he was garbed in a fawn cloak complete with silver clasp, fawn breeches and patent shoes with buckles.

'Guten Tag meine Freunde,' he said brightly. 'Would either one of you gentlemen be Herr ...' He paused to consult a piece of paper. 'Herr Crusty Grogan?'

Boff blew his nose to stop himself laughing.

'You mean Rusty,' Paul grinned.

'Ja, zat is good. Crusty Rusty. He is here, nein?'

'He is here, *yes*.' Paul indicated Grogan skulking in the office doorway.

'Zat is ze owner?'

'No, Major Palmer's the owner. Grogan's the head lad.'

Von Sternberg brushed up the ends of his moustache. 'Excuse me, but my Engleesh is not good. Is zat ze man who is responsible for looking after ze horses?'

Paul nodded.

'Wunderbar! And you mein Herr – you are ze jockey who rides zem?'

'Some of them.'

'You are...' His eyes dropped to the paper. 'Charlie Carver, ja?'

'Paul Steel.'

'Steel?' He sniffed. 'I do not have Steel written here. It cannot be you who will ride my magnificent Alaric.'

Paul snapped his fingers. 'Alaric – that's the German entry in the Grand National. Now I understand –'

'You understand nothing, Herr Steel! You insult Alaric by calling him German. He is an *Austrian* horse, made – I mean born in my native Austria.'

'I see,' Paul was having difficulty in keeping a straight face. 'Well, I wish you luck.'

Von Sternberg gave a derisive grunt. 'Alaric does not rely on luck. He will crush ze opposition into little pieces. He is ze greatest horse ever to set foot on Engleesh soil.'

Boff took a deep breath to steady himself. 'I beg your pardon, Doctor von St – St – Sternberg,' he stammered, 'but you happen to be looking at Mylor, *our* Grand National entry.'

'Zis chestnut horse is yours?' He stepped back, examining Mylor critically. 'Ja, he's not bad. For an Engleesh animal perhaps even good. But against my Alaric he looks – how you say in racing jargon – a selling plater.'

I wasn't too sure what that meant, but gathering from Paul's expression it wasn't exactly a compliment.

'Are you an expert then, Doctor?' The jockey challenged him, springing to Mylor's defence. 'I've been in racing since I was fifteen and I know a good horse when I see one. Believe me, I'm seeing one now.'

Boff threw out his chest and grinned triumphantly. I patted Mylor's neck proudly, very glad we had Paul on our side.

Von Sternberg pursed his lips and ran his tongue over the bristles of his moustache. 'I will convince you, Herr Steel,' he said arrogantly, then he turned on his heel and marched smartly towards Grogan.

'Blasted cheek!' Boff's breath hissed through his teeth.

'I'd better tell the Major he's arrived,' Paul said. 'Wait here.'

I watched Grogan exchange words with von Sternberg. They shook hands and then the Doctor opened his black bag and began pointing at whatever it contained. Grogan kept nodding enthusiastically and rubbing his hands. Eventually they were joined by Charlie Carver and this resulted in a huddled conference. They were too far away to be heard, but the sly grin on Grogan's face was enough to tell me they were up to no good.

Mylor dipped his head and began pawing the cobbles with a foreleg. I didn't take much notice at first because I guessed he was just impatient to get home.

It was only when the leg movement became more frenzied that it dawned on me he was trying to tell us something – or at least, somebody was.

'Morse code!' It suddenly clicked. I swung to Boff. 'Mylor's talking to us in Morse code!'

'Huh?' His eyes flickered uncertainly. 'H-he can't be. He hasn't got a communication circuit.'

'Then it's–' I stopped myself and concentrated hard.

Tap scrape, scrape tap, scrape scrape tap, tap, tap scrape tap tap.

'A – N – G – E – L!'

Boff blinked, whispered, 'She's inside Mylor.'

I grinned with relief and leaned towards the ear-mikes. 'Are you all right?'

Mylor's golden mane fluttered as he lifted and dropped his neck.

'She must have switched him to manual,' Boff said.

'Who let you out of the tack-room?' I asked.

Mylor's hoof lifted and a series of taps and scrapes spelled out the words: Ought did.

Of course! I pounded my fist into my palm as it all began to fit together. The stable lad must have heard her moving about when he went to mix up the second batch of gruel. He'd let her out and probably shown her a back way to Fireball's box. She'd opened the chest-hatch and climbed in while we were checking the tack-room. I guessed that Ought had since made himself scarce fearing Angel's detection by Grogan.

'What do you think he's got in his bag?' Boff's eyes grew thoughtful, curious, as he studied the threesome.

I shrugged. 'A stethoscope maybe, some bottles –'

'He doesn't have to be a Doctor of Medicine. I think it's more likely he's a Doctor of Philosophy.'

'Which means?'

'He has great knowledge of the causes and laws of

all things. Natural science and stuff like that.'

'Not the sort of person to have much in common with Grogan,' I commented.

'To have nothing in common with Grogan, unless...'

'Unless?'

'No,' Boff dismissed the thought. 'I'm on the wrong tack, Roger. It would be too much of a coincidence.'

I didn't like being left in the air, but as Paul was returning with Major Palmer, I didn't have any choice. I instructed Angel to switch Mylor back on instinct and then I began leading the horse towards the Rice trailer.

Alaric was making his exit from the multi-coloured travelling box. There was a lot of stamping and whinnying, and Grogan who had entered with a head collar and halter seemed to have no control over the bad-tempered animal.

'Be careful with zat horse!' von Sternberg shouted. 'He is highly strung and must be handled with goat gloves.'

'Kid gloves,' Carver corrected him.

'Kid? Goat? What difference?' He pushed Carver towards the ramp. 'When I want an Engleesh lesson I will ask you – now help Herr Grogan!'

Two pairs of hands wrestled with the halter and eventually Alaric was coaxed from the box to the yard. He was every inch as big as Mylor, every bit as well muscled; black as coal apart from a small white star between his eyes – and what strange eyes they were too. There was something positively evil about them. A shiver ran the length of my body as he turned his head to look at me. His whole appearance was one of menace. His powerful stance, the impatient swish of his tail, the way his nostrils ridged and twitched with each breath – they oozed hostility.

Mylor could also feel it; he was getting restive and excited. 'Easy boy, easy,' I whispered, nursing him to the trailer.

Von Sternberg kept peering into his little black bag, constantly fiddling with whatever lay inside. He sighed loudly in exasperation and his expression became rather complicated. 'Something is upsetting my Alaric,' he announced suddenly. 'There is a power source nearby, nein? Some electric cables perhaps, or a generator?'

Major Palmer's face tightened. 'We have nothing like that here. This is a stable, Doctor, not a plant for producing electricity.'

'Nevertheless my Alaric feels it. I do not lie. Look at ze way he behaves. Zat is not normal.'

'That's bad temperament,' Paul put in.

The Doctor's face reddened. 'Zat's not bad temperament – zat's electricity?'

'Rubbish. A horse can't be affected in that way.'

The Doctor's face reddened a bit more. I thought he was going to explode. He closed his eyes for a second or two, fighting to keep a grip on his rising temper. 'I don't expect you to understand, Herr Steel, but Alaric is a highly sensitive animal. Atmospheric disturbances can unbalance him – make him edgy.'

Paul looked unconvinced. He simply turned to the Major and shrugged.

I glanced at Boff. 'It must be Mylor,' I said. 'His solar power is interfering with Alaric's...' My voice straggled away as I realised what I was saying.

'You've got it, Roger,' Boff moistened his lips and looked grim. 'Doctor von Sternberg is here to try and gain membership to the International Inventors' Institute. Alaric isn't a real horse at all – he's a machine.'

Any numbness my brain might have been feeling

was instantly cleared the moment Alaric threw up his head and wrenched the halter from Grogan's hands. There was a loud snort and a flurry of hooves as the big horse launched himself at me.

'*Look out, Roger!*' Paul shouted the warning. He tried blocking Alaric's path but the horse bored into him, tossing him away like a skittle.

Mylor reared, forcing me to release my grip. I went spinning towards the Rice trailer and hit it pretty hard. The impact knocked the breath from my body and I just stood there, winded and gasping for air. I was a perfect target for the big black horse, but it wasn't me he was after. His teeth flashed and his eyes rolled wildly as he turned his attack to Mylor. He'd discovered the energy source and he wanted to destroy it. I gritted my teeth, desperately worried about Angel, hoping she'd had enough sense to fasten her safety harness.

'Grogan!' the Major bellowed. 'Get control of that horse!'

A nerve fluttered in Grogan's mottled face. He was staring fixedly at the heaving black stallion and hardly seemed to hear. He ran the back of his hand across his lips and began shouting for Ought.

Von Sternberg was still fiddling with his little black bag. I guessed it contained some sort of transmitter for controlling Alaric's movements. It wasn't having any effect. He threw his hat to the ground and began stamping on it. 'Sie dummer Kerl!' he yelled at Grogan. 'Sie blöder Hund!'

Paul came towards me clutching his side. The sleeve of his shirt was torn and he had a smear of blood on his face. 'Are you all right?' he asked shakily.

I nodded, wincing as Alaric's hooves thudded into Mylor's back like a battering ram.

Doctor von Sternberg was still fiddling with his little black bag. I winced as Alaric's hooves thudded into Mylor's back like a battering ram.

Spider was darting around and barking and in danger of being trampled underfoot. Boff dashed forward, grabbed his collar and whisked him into his arms. He circled around the Range-Rover and joined us.

'Mylor's going to get damaged,' he said breathlessly. 'I wish I'd fixed that faulty stab–' He stopped on seeing Paul.

'Damaged?' Paul blinked. 'That's a strange word to use.'

'I – I mean hurt,' Boff covered quickly. 'He could get badly h-hurt.'

'He seems to be holding his own.'

Mylor's hindquarters bunched and his forelegs began threshing at Alaric's neck. I thought of the tremendous power being supplied by the hydraulic fluid as it surged through Mylor's plastic veins at three thousand pounds' pressure. It was certainly having an effect on the black stallion. Although locked like two warriors in an arena, Alaric seemed to be weakening under the punishing blows. His hindlegs were skidding on the cobbles and he was being forced backwards. Von Sternberg looked stricken.

'Sind sie vorsichtig!' He shouted the command to Alaric. I'd learned enough German at school to know he was ordering the horse to take care.

Ought appeared on the scene. Grogan spotted him and yelled, 'Get in there and break them 'orses up!'

The boy gulped visibly but he ran forward, chasing Alaric's halter as it snaked along the ground. He caught the end and began looping it round his hand and elbow. As the slack was gathered up so he was drawn nearer and nearer to the black stallion's tossing head. Ought might not be able to make decisions but he could certainly carry out instructions. I suspected he was far more frightened of Rusty Grogan than he was of the horse.

'Give him a hand!' Major Palmer ordered.

Grogan looked tense and then inclined his head stiffly. He grabbed Ought round the waist to stop the boy being physically lifted off the ground but it wasn't enough to combat the power in Alaric's neck. Charlie held Grogan and all three were hoisted like puppets on a string.

'*Die Idioten!*' Von Sternberg slapped his forehead with his palm.

Mylor's forelegs were still lashing out in a fearful rhythm. Blow was exchanged for blow and although Alaric was considerably weakened he had no intention of giving up the fight.

'That head collar's going to snap,' Paul warned. 'If that aggressive beast gets loose...'

I looked at him and for the first time I saw fear in his eyes. I wiped the sleeve of my jerkin across my face and tried to think. Alaric wouldn't stop attacking Mylor until the electricity which clashed with his circuits had ceased. An idea flashed across my brain. My hands were shaking as I cupped them to my mouth and yelled, 'Switch off the solar-storage!'

Mylor's ear-mikes relayed the message to Angel and the black stallion's response was immediate. It was as if his savage, uncontrollable nature had been transformed. His eyes and tongue rolled momentarily, then he wrenched himself clear of Mylor. As Ought, Grogan and Carver tumbled to the ground in a tangled heap, Major Palmer stepped forward to take charge of the halter. Alaric put up no resistance. He just stood calmly, his head lolling between his shoulder blades, his flanks trembling from fatigue.

Paul clutched Mylor's head collar, steadied him. 'What on earth did you say?' He shot me a quizzical look. 'I didn't quite catch –'

'I – I insulted him,' I said quickly. 'I can't imagine why it had such an effect.'

'Neither can I. What was it?'

'Well...'

Boff who had been chewing his lip came to my rescue. 'Shove off you sore squabbler!' he announced with feeling.

It was a good spur of the moment cover-up. 'Y-yes,' I swallowed and nodded. 'That's it, that's what I shouted.'

Paul didn't look particularly convinced, but he accepted it with a shrug of his shoulders and led Mylor into the trailer.

Von Sternberg was staring at me in a hard, icy way. I was pretty sure he'd heard my instruction to Angel and it was more than probable that he knew what it meant. Had he guessed that Mylor was a piece of sophisticated machinery – just as Boff and I had realised that of Alaric? I didn't hang around to find out. Paul was about to fasten the ramp and I wanted to check on Angel before we got under way.

'I'll do that,' I volunteered. 'I'd like to give Mylor the once-over just in case he's been hurt.'

'Sure,' Paul smiled amicably. 'I'll wait for you in the Range-Rover.'

Rusty Grogan, Charlie Carver, the Doctor and Major Palmer were all down at the far end of the yard. Alaric was being allocated a loose-box and they were all far too interested in the horse to be worrying about me. I slipped into the trailer, pressed Mylor's forelock button, then crept under his ribcage. The chest-hatch swung open as I pushed hard with my fingertips.

Angel was strapped in the front seat. She turned to look at me, her face puckering slightly, traces of dried salt glistening on her cheeks. I climbed in and hugged her close.

'You were great,' I said softly. 'Not only a super sister but part of a team. And that's what we all are, Angel – part of a team.'

She tried to smile. 'I think that Austrian man heard what you said about the solar-storage. I think he's suspicious of Mylor.'

'He's got good reason to be. Alaric's a machine, too.'

'So that's why...'

'It was upsetting his circuits. If I hadn't yelled out then the horses might have smashed each other to bits. The sooner we get away from this place the better. Do you mind staying in here until we reach Parkway?'

'Must I?'

'Paul would ask a host of awkward questions if you just suddenly appeared.'

'I suppose so,' she ran her fingers through her straw-coloured hair and uttered a sigh. 'It's just that I'm so hungry I could –'

'Eat a horse?' I said, grinning.

Her old smile returned. It was good to see. I carefully closed the chest-hatch and brought Mylor back to life by thumbing the tiny red button. I covered it with his forelock and edged my way out of the trailer.

'Talking to yourself, then?' Ought's voice startled me as I lifted the ramp.

I turned, looked at him blankly.

'Just now,' he went on. 'I thought I heard you talking to someone.'

'Only Mylor,' I said. 'I often chat to him ... to calm him down.'

'Oh,' he peered past the trailer to the Range-Rover, 'only I think there's something you ought to know.'

'If it's about Angel I know already. I'd like to thank you.'

'Is she . . . ?'

'Safe and hidden where nobody can find her.'

'Rusty Grogan must never learn that I let her out,' he said guardedly. 'Promise me you won't tell anyone, not even Paul.'

'I promise.'

'Well, I suppose it's goodbye, then.' He spat on the palm of his hand, wiped it on his jeans and held it out for me to shake.

'Thanks,' I said once again.

As he padded slowly away, no doubt thinking about all the 'oughts' he should have either done or be doing. I had a strong hunch we'd be seeing him again soon. I secured the ramp's safety clips and walked towards the Range-Rover.

'I've decided to accept your proposition,' Paul wound down his side window and smiled easily.

'Proposition?' I wasn't thinking all that clearly.

'The Grand National,' Boff's voice bubbled with excitement. 'Paul's agreed to ride Mylor.'

'That's great,' I gazed at him enquiringly. 'What made you change your mind?'

'A certain Doctor von Sternberg. I'd hate to see him pick up the prize.'

'Alaric's got plenty of spirit. I think he'll take a lot of beating.'

'Aren't you forgetting something, Roger?' Paul started the engine, then looked at me with a glint of humour in his eyes. 'We're entering Mylor – and nothing can beat the most powerful horse in the world.'

Chapter Five

It was the following morning and Angel had prepared us a hearty breakfast of eggs, bacon and fried bread. The Professor tucked in hungrily, pausing between mouthfuls to consult various books that were piled high by his plate and to compliment my sister on her cooking ability.

'This is truly excellent, young lady...' He broke off suddenly, tapped his finger against a book page, and beamed at Boff. 'You were right, Algernon. I've found him in here and this verifies your suspicions.'

'Found who, Gramps?' A forkful of bacon hovered half way to Boff's mouth.

'Von Sternberg, my boy. He's listed in the *Inventor's Who's Who*. He's a Doctor of Philosophy and a Bachelor of Science. A formidable candidate for membership of the Institute, yes indeed. Studied at the University of Vienna from nineteen fifty...' The Professor rambled on, quoting from the page, reeling out words so long that it made you feel dizzy just listening to them.

'So he's got plenty up top,' I said, as the Professor closed the book.

'Up top, Roger?'

'Brains.'

'Brains? Yes, yes, indeed. I should imagine that his horse has been built with the greatest amount of precision.'

'He didn't like Mylor,' Angel complained, offering Boff a second helping of eggs. 'It was awful when they were fighting.'

'It was the solar-storage, Gramps,' Boff said. 'It caused the Doctor's horse to go haywire.'

'Most puzzling.' Two vertical furrows ran between the Professor's wispy eyebrows.

'You should have heard what he called Grogan,' I grinned. I stood up, shook my fist in the air and deepened my voice. 'Sie Idiot! Sie dummer Kerl!'

'Plus zis, zat and ze other,' Boff smiled hugely.

'How about zoot?' I winked at him.

'He wouldn't dare,' Boff mocked. 'That word's strictly the property of Angel Young.'

'Oh, funny, ha, ha.' Angel pulled a face and switched the second helping of eggs from Boff's plate to the Professor's.

'Hey...!'

'Don't be so noisy, Algernon.' The Professor, who hadn't seen what had happened, looked up from his book. He frowned at Boff and smiled at Angel. 'Third helpings? Good gracious, young lady, you're spoiling me.'

'But, Gramps...' Boff protested.

'What *is* the matter, Algernon?'

'You've got my...'

'Yes?' The Professor sliced the eggs in two and dunked his fried bread in the yolk.

'It doesn't matter,' Boff murmured weakly.

Baffled, the Professor returned to his book. 'The name Alaric is German in origin,' he announced. 'It means ruler of all.'

'Not quite all,' I stated. 'He didn't get the better of Mylor.'

'True my boy, very true. But the Doctor's bound to make improvements. How do you think Alaric's operated?'

'By remote control. The Doctor carries this little black bag with him. I think it's packed with electronic gadgetry.'

The Professor nodded and wiped egg from his face with a napkin.

'Charlie Carver rides the horse,' Angel piped up, cracking more eggs in the frying pan. It was a huge stove with hot-plates that were heated by coal, and it in no way resembled the modern electric cooker we had at home. 'He's as big a crook as Grogan,' she added, 'so there's bound to be some jiggery-pokery.'

'Jiggery-pokery?' The Professor's eyebrows arched.

'Yes, unfair play. If they've guessed that Mylor's a machine then I think they'll harm him ... try to put him out of action.'

'Nonsense, young lady, that would be most unethical. Doctor von Sternberg would have no part of it.'

'I'm not so sure, Gramps,' Boff remarked, draining his cocoa. 'Perhaps we should think about tightening up on security.'

The Professor sighed and put his fingertips together. 'You've been watching too much television, my boy. You make the competition sound like a game of cops and robbers.'

Angel ducked under a low ceiling beam and served a much relieved Boff with his second helping of eggs. 'Mylor was snatched,' she reminded the Professor, 'and I was locked up in a tack-room.'

'A dreadful experience,' he agreed, 'but that had nothing to do with the Doctor. He's a prospective Institute member and therefore bound by a code of conduct. I'm sure he's a professional man of good character who wouldn't dream of stooping to that sort of skulduggery.'

Angel flicked me a glance which meant 'Oh, wouldn't he just' and I countered with one which meant 'Yes, but try convincing the Professor.' Her blue eyes softened and she smiled. Spider padded back and forth by his bowl. Every now and then he would stop, wag his tail and look at us expectantly. Angel reminded him that he didn't get his meat and biscuits until lunch time. He whined, covered his eyes with his paws and put on his usual act of looking thoroughly miserable.

'You're a cheat!' Angel pretended to scold him. She clicked her tongue in mild annoyance and began collecting the table scraps. He perked up immediately.

'Delicious, young lady, delicious.' The Professor blew out his stomach and patted it contentedly. 'I don't know how we ever managed before you came.'

'We didn't,' Boff commented. 'It was always cornflakes or something out of a tin.'

Angel handed me a dish mop and Boff a tea towel. She filled the big old-fashioned sink with water, squeezed in some liquid soap, and then stood looking at us with arms folded. Boff and I exchanged glances. We got the message.

The thought of washing up didn't appeal to Professor Parkway. He eased his way quietly clear of the table and towards a corner cabinet. He issued us each with a set of freshly laundered overalls and asked us to meet him in the workshop when we'd finished.

'Aren't you going to lend a hand, Gramps?' Boff raised questioning eyebrows.

'I'd like to but –' He caught his breath sharply as he glanced at his watch. 'I haven't the time, my boy. Must fix that faulty stabiliser, yes, indeed. Besides, you know the old saying about too many cooks.'

'What about many hands make light work?' Boff countered.

'Never heard of it,' he murmured inadequately,

edging towards the door. 'I – I'll see you at the workshop ... must get on ... lots to do ...'

He nearly tripped over Spider's bowl of breakfast scraps in his hurry to get out. Our little cairn barked angrily. We all laughed.

The huge fleecy clouds which dominated the sky for most of the morning broke up in the early afternoon. Birds sang in the high branches overlooking the workshop and Mylor's solar-storage system soaked up the sun's rays. When the energy indicator registered fully-charged, Boff pressed a button on a control console and the powder-blue sky slid slowly from view as the workshop's electronic roof closed.

'How goes it, Gramps?' Boff switched on the interior lights.

'Surgery completed,' the Professor announced, wriggling from the chest-hatch. His face was smudged with oil and his spectacles were hanging by one ear. He fixed them in place and squinted at the object in his right hand. 'Mylor wouldn't have jumped any Grand National fences with this,' he added gravely.

'Is that the stabiliser?' I asked.

'Indeed, Roger, yes indeed.'

'How exactly does it work?'

'It helps to keep Mylor balanced. He has one at the front and one at the rear. It's a gyroscopic device in which a flywheel rotates ... well, it's all very technical, my boy.'

'Is the new one fitted?' Boff queried.

The Professor nodded and handed me a screwdriver. 'Put the cover plate back on, Roger, and we'll take Mylor out for a test.'

The chest-hatch treads were a trifle greasy and I lost my footing on the top one. The hawser stopped me from taking a tumble but my hair tangled around the pneumatic dampener and I squealed as the roots took the strain.

'If you're going to have hair as long as a girl's then use their method for keeping it tidy,' Boff chuckled appreciatively as he freed my blond strands. As I massaged my scalp he indicated Angel who was wearing her hair in a pony-tail. It swung neatly round her ears as she polished Mylor's coat with a stable rubber. Boff's smile deepened. 'Can I lend you an elastic band, Roger?'

I scowled at him and was about to reply but the wailing note of the main gate siren beat me to it.

'An uninvited visitor.' The Professor's head shot up, his eyes diamond bright.

Boff motioned to a wall-mounted monitor. He unclipped a hand-mike and flicked a switch. The picture rolled then steadied. A figure wearing a chequered open-necked shirt with sleeves dragged back to the elbows was staring undecidedly at the maze. The camera zoomed in to show the rugged features of Paul Steel.

'Hello, Paul,' Boff's lips moved against the mike, 'this is a surprise.'

'You've surprised me,' he said. 'Where are you?'

'At the house. Have you come for a visit?'

'I'd like to see Roger.'

'He's here. Stay put and I'll send transport.' Boff stabbed a forefinger on a button marked *Mazemobile*.

'Is it Paul?' Angel left her grooming and dashed to the screen. 'Oh, yes!' she breathed excitedly, then visibly checked her emotions when she saw we were grinning at her.

'Your sister's got a crush on him,' Boff said.

'Her Prince Charming,' I agreed.

'Don't be so silly,' she flushed then stammered, 'I – I admire him, that's all.'

The Professor unbuttoned his overalls and stepped out of them. He straightened his knitted tie and pulled a handkerchief from the pocket of his hairy tweed suit. 'Mr Steel mustn't see us like this,' he said, rubbing the oil smears from his face. 'He believes Mylor's real and we dare not give him cause to think otherwise. Algernon, climb in the chest-hatch and take the horse to the south field as quickly as possible.'

'*Me*, Gramps?' Boff gaped. 'But I'm not the pilot.'

'You'll manage, my boy.'

'I'm not so sure. I –'

'You won't have to do anything – just trot around a bit when you get there. It's Roger Mr Steel has come to see, so I can't send him.'

'Oh, crikey.' Boff took a gasping breath as he made his way up the treads.

The Professor closed the chest-hatch then glanced at the monitor. Paul had separated the two halves of the mazemobile and was climbing in.

'He's carrying something.' Angel's eyes expressed surprise. 'I think it's ... golly, it is. A saddle and bridle!'

With news like that I expected the chest-hatch to open and for Boff to make a flying exit. When he didn't it became pretty obvious that Mylor's ear-mikes hadn't yet been switched on. I looked worriedly at Angel who in turn looked worriedly at the Professor. He clamped his pipe between his teeth and waggled it up and down. 'Oh, dear me,' were the only words he could manage.

Mylor's powerful legs suddenly sprang into life and his aluminium shoes rat-tatted on the chessboard floor. Boff was at the controls.

'Go easy with the –' My voice was sliced off as the horse did a jerky leap forward, cannoning past us and out of the workshop. '... pace-selector,' I added weakly as the dust settled.

The Professor rubbed his forehead and looked anxious as he strode towards the armoured steel door. We quickly removed our overalls and joined him. The metal shutter rattled and fell, blocking the workshop from view. We reached the old timbered house just in time to meet the mazemobile.

'Phew!' Paul grinned and parted the shell. 'I've ridden in some weird contraptions in my time, but this takes the biscuit.'

'You remembered the rhyme,' Angel said.

'Sure I did. It's one of those things you never –' He paused, blinked. 'Hey, Angel, you're back. How...?'

Angel smiled prettily and launched into a story we'd carefully rehearsed last night. She told Paul the version that he'd suggested to us – the bolt was old, it hadn't been properly locked, and by kicking the door she'd managed to jiggle it free.

He mulled that over, then said, 'I figured that a possibility at the time, but how did you refasten the bolt? And why didn't you let us know you were safe?'

'I was terribly frightened of Grogan. All I wanted to do was get back to Parkway, so I walked to the main road and caught a bus.' She flattened her palms against the mazemobile and told a final white lie to protect Ought. 'The bolt was easy really. I levered it back with the prong of a pitchfork.'

He slapped his thigh. 'Easy when you know how. Hell, am I glad you're okay.'

Her cheeks reddened. She lowered her eyes.

The Professor gave a discreet little cough and I realised I was forgetting my manners. I made the introductions.

'Great horse you've got, Professor,' Paul enthused. 'I can't wait to get a leg either side of him.'

'A leg...?'

82

'Ride him.' He patted the saddle, rattled the bridle. 'When we were driving back yesterday, Roger mentioned your practice fences. He said for me to come over in the middle of the week, but I've never been one for dragging my heels.'

'So you intend...?'

'Just for half an hour. A few good jumps so I can get the feel of the horse.'

The Professor's face shadowed. His only response was a vague, 'Yes, indeed ... I suppose so ... If you must, you must.'

We packed ourselves into the mazemobile and the Professor programmed the vehicle to take us to the south field.

'Poor Boff,' Angel murmured as the engine crooned into life.

'Boff?' Paul's eyes expressed concern. 'I noticed he wasn't here. Is anything wrong?'

'No, everything's fine.' The smile I was attempting hung tightly on my lips. 'What Angel means is ... well, he'll miss out on all the excitement.'

The Professor gave me a sideward glance and grunted. Certainly 'missing out' was the last thing his grandson would be doing.

'Our parents might be ringing today,' Angel covered convincingly, 'so as you asked to see Roger, Boff volunteered to man the telephone.'

The mazemobile was rapidly approaching the south field. It sped past hedgerows, trundled over uneven areas of heather and bracken and bounced and rattled as its little wheels carried it over a cattle grid. A five-bar gate loomed ahead. Mylor stood majestically behind it, ears pricked, watching our arrival with keen interest.

As we began to slow, Paul whispered, 'I wanted to see you, Roger, because you're the oldest. It's about the saddle Alaric's wearing in the National.'

'Saddle?'

'It belongs to Doctor von Sternberg and Charlie Carver's quite happy to use it.'

I looked at him blankly.

'Jockeys always use their own saddles, Roger. They get used to the feel and the balance. Charlie Carver's got three good ones, so why on earth...'

'Would he ride with the Doctor's?' I supplied, rubbing my chin. 'He'd have to have one heck of a good reason.'

'Beats me,' Paul shrugged.

'Have you noticed anything special about it?'

'They won't let me near it. Now they know I'm riding Mylor I'm considered one of the enemy. I'll tell you something though, that Alaric's a flyer. I watched him on the training track this morning and can he move fast.'

I said as casually as I could, 'I suppose the Doctor was there with his little black bag.'

'Oh, he was there all right – but no bag. Funny thing about that, he only seems to carry it when Charlie's not riding the horse.'

Or when the saddle's not on, I thought. It was all very blurred and mysterious. Our only hope of finding something out was to ask Ought to investigate. I made a mental note to contact him tomorrow.

The mazemobile slowed to a halt. Professor Parkway separated the shell and we all clambered out. Mylor's eyes were following me as I strolled to the gate. I imagined Boff glued to the video, watching in horror as he spotted the tack in Paul's hand.

'These practice fences are superb.' The jockey leaned against a lichen-covered post and surveyed the layout. 'We'll certainly be able to put Mylor through his paces here, eh, Professor?'

'Yes.' The Professor's pipe rattled nervously against his teeth. 'Yes, indeed.'

Paul grinned at me, the wind tossing his thick hair over his forehead. He fixed his helmet in position and fastened the chin-strap.

I tried a carefree smile, but nothing happened. Mylor's large trusting eyes hadn't left my face and it was all very unnerving.

'Don't expect too much, Paul,' Angel said, slipping the bit into Mylor's mouth and gently easing his ears through the browband and crown piece of the bridle. 'He can be stubborn at times ... he might refuse to jump.'

'Now don't you fret yourself, little lady.' Paul threw his saddle over Mylor's back and buckled the girths. 'He's a fine big horse, rangy and tailor-made for fences such as these. Has he a good engine?'

'E-engine?' Angel faltered.

'A racing expression. It means will he stay the distance – have enough steam to last four and a half miles?'

Fully charged, Mylor had twice that range and then a bit more besides. Angel knew this but she said carefully, 'He doesn't tire easily. The longer the race the better it suits him.'

'Great.' Paul sounded confident as he hoisted himself into the saddle. He tapped his heels against Mylor's flanks. 'Okay, boy, let's see what you can do.'

I closed my eyes hardly daring to look. I heard Angel catch her breath on a gasp as Mylor cantered away. 'I've got my fingers crossed, Boff,' she murmured.

The rhythm of hooves quickened. The canter changed into a gallop and my heart began thumping as Paul headed for the first jump. Five seconds ... six seconds ... seven. The turf under my feet seemed to shake. Eight seconds ... nine ... a deathly hush as Mylor lifted, and then...

'He's over!' Angel began jogging up and down with excitement.

My eyelids sprang open. I grinned and relaxed a little.

The Professor was massaging his temples. 'A beautiful landing,' he admitted. 'The impact-absorbers in Mylor's legs are working better than I'd hoped. Thank goodness I completed the stabiliser refit.'

We all watched, mesmerised as Mylor jumped the second. I found myself subconsciously giving Boff instructions, but of course he couldn't hear them, and anyway he was doing incredibly well on his own.

It was a spectacular leap; high and perfectly timed. Our chestnut wonder horse took it as easily as if it was a two-foot pole in a pony club gymkhana. His mane and tail were flying, his burnished coat glistening, his white feet flashing. Paul crouched low over the withers as he headed for jump number three – the ditch.

'Well done, Boff!' Angel's excited fingers snapped the band securing her neatly gathered hair. Her blonde locks tumbled on to the shoulders of her cheesecloth blouse. Her eyes were aglow. 'Look at the way Paul rides,' she breathed wistfully. 'Isn't he wonderful, Roger. Isn't he just ... just wonderful.'

'Wonderful,' I echoed, giving her my soppy look. 'Boff was right, you have got a crush on him.'

'Hooey!' She poked out the little pink tip of her tongue.

'He jumped the ditch like a veteran,' the Professor was saying, 'another two fences and he'll be at Becher's Brook.'

'Becher's...' Angel's slim body stiffened. 'Isn't that where a lot of them fall? I've seen it on television. It's

It was a spectacular leap; high and perfectly timed. Our chestnut wonder horse took it as if it was a two-foot pole in a pony club gymkhana.

horribly high.'

'And my replica fence is just as high,' the Professor attested. 'Same specification and faultless down to the finest detail. It's a very long drop, yes indeed.'

Mylor sailed over fences four and five with thrilling fluency. Boff timed the landings to perfection but that didn't stop my heart being in my mouth as our horse headed for Becher's Brook.

'Yeah, boy!' Paul urged Mylor with vocal commands and by relaxing his snug hold on the reins. Boff immediately responded by lengthening Mylor's stride. They were going a blistering gallop.

'It—it's too fast,' Angel's voice sounded breathy, uncertain. 'He'll lose control.'

'Throttle back, Boff,' I found myself saying. 'You're not watching your speed-indicator needle. You're going to –'

Shock held me silent. For the space of an eye blink Mylor wallowed sharply to the left as Boff realised his mistake. It was too late to correct. Paul lost his forward position and Mylor jumped high – unbelievably high. He cleared Becher's by at least two feet of daylight and as he made his descent Paul was catapulted out of the saddle.

'Zoot!' Angel's hands flew to her mouth.

Mylor landed awkwardly but the stabilisers stopped him from falling. Paul wasn't so lucky. He somersaulted high in the air and hit the ground with a flesh-bruising thump. I saw him sit up painfully and wince as he rubbed his shoulder. Angel and the Professor dashed over to help him.

Mylor was making a bee-line for me. The reins flapped loosely around his powerful neck as he slowed. I expected Boff to operate the dead-stop mechanism as he drew level, but he veered past seeking the cover of one of the fences. All I could see was the fine flare of Mylor's nostrils as he peered over the top of the gorse dressing.

I ran behind the fence, freed off the girths and opened the chest-hatch. Boff wobbled his way down the treads looking a trifle green.

'N-never again,' he stammered. 'I – I'm not a pilot, I'm an engineer.'

I smothered a grin. 'How are you feeling?'

'Terrible. My stomach ... oooh, don't mention it.'

'You'd better climb back before Paul sees you.'

'*Back?*' His voice was strangled. 'I need the air. Put Mylor on instinct, I – I'll walk to the house.'

'It's a long walk.'

'I'll manage ... I think I'm –' He clamped a hand to his mouth and walked dizzily to the fence. 'E-excuse me, Roger,' he added and was promptly sick.

I took off the saddle and bridle, closed the chest-hatch and depressed the forelock button. Mylor's instincts clicked on. He snorted, nudged me playfully, then flicked his heels in a swanky display of showmanship. He streaked off towards the far side of the field, his ears pricked and lively, his mane streaming.

Boff tottered away too. His face wasn't green any more, just unhealthily white. I murmured a hasty see-you-later, and hotfooted it back to the Professor.

Paul's shirt was muddy and blotched with sweat stains across the shoulders. 'That's quite a horse you've got,' he was saying. 'I had difficulty controlling him – it's almost as if he has an unbendable will of his own.'

'Are you hurt?' I asked anxiously.

'A little shaken. I'm all right.'

'That was an awful tumble at Becher's.' Angel's voice was the barest murmur.

'I've never known a horse jump so high. He was flying – literally flying. He's a descendant of Pegasus,

I'm sure of it.'

The Professor cleared his throat. 'Tea?' he suggested.

'Tea?' The sudden change of topic made Paul blink.

'Everything seems better over tea, yes indeed. We'll take the mazemobile back to the house and Angel can put the kettle on.'

'You can try one of my scones,' Angel cooed, giving him a special smile.

'You've got a deal.' Paul unclipped his helmet. 'How can I refuse?'

'You can't,' the Professor said. 'Angel's scones are lighter than air. You have to keep a firm grip on them or they're liable to float away.'

The wrinkles creased around Paul's deep grey eyes. 'They sound a little like Mylor,' he grinned.

We all went to bed early that night. It had been an exhausting day in more ways than one and I was very glad to snuggle under a warm eiderdown and drift blissfully to sleep.

I would have stayed that way had it not been for Spider leaping on to my bed in the early hours. I awoke with a jolt as he pressed his moist nose against my cheek. Once he had my attention he darted to the window and began scratching at the candy-striped wallpaper.

'Heck, Spider,' I complained, peering blearily at the luminous hands of my alarm, 'it's two o'clock in the morning!'

His little feet scrabbled some more. Any moment he was going to start barking.

'Stop that!' I scolded, throwing back the bedclothes. 'You'll wake up the whole –'

Something flashed in the corner of my eye. I turned

towards the window and glimpsed the beam from a torch. It wavered for a few seconds illuminating the bright green of the maze and then began moving in the direction of the workshop.

Intruders? The thought flashed through my mind. I grabbed my fleecy-lined jacket and pulled it on over my pyjamas. The zip jammed against one of the buttons and I stubbed my toe against the wardrobe as I struggled into my shoes. Amazingly, Boff in the bed opposite remained asleep through all my muttered curses and Spider's constant toing and froing. If he'd woken I'd have asked for his help, but seeing he was unwell and dead to the world I decided to leave him in peace.

Spider ran on ahead as I tiptoed across the landing. The floorboards were old and had a nasty habit of creaking, so I was especially careful as I passed Angel's and the Professor's bedrooms. They were both in darkness and I could hear the Professor snoring loudly. I made my way down the staircase, rubbed the weariness from my eyes and followed Spider through the hall to the front door.

A cold night breeze ruffled my jacket on the slow, cautious walk to the workshop. The moon's glow filtered through scudding clouds, stretching shadows to an unnatural angle and giving the wind-tossed trees the look of something seen in a nightmare. Spider wasn't feeling so bold any more. He padded by my side, not wishing to take the lead.

If there was somebody here then why hadn't the siren gone off? How had they managed the maze and...? The thoughts disappeared and my breathing quickened as we came within sight of the workshop. The metal shutter was up. The illuminated thumb-print button was broken and some strange gadget had been clamped just above it.

I stepped inside, went to reach for the light switch then hesitated. I heard a sound like a breathy grunt and I tensed. Butterflies swarmed in my stomach. Spider sensed danger, growled and backed up.

'Who's there?' I challenged in as brave a voice as I could manage.

Silence.

My eyes were getting accustomed to the darkness. I could just make out the vague outline of ... I blinked ... It couldn't be ...

My finger touched the light switch.

Mylor! No – no – no!

He was standing in the centre of the chessboard floor. The chest-hatch was open and ripped wires and cables dangled over the treads like spaghetti. A hacksaw lay nearby, its ugly blade glinting at me. He must have been left on instinct because his eyes swivelled to look at me.

'M-Mylor,' I called to him gently, waiting and watching to see how much of his circuitry had been damaged.

He didn't respond at first, but then slowly – very, very slowly his haunches flexed and he turned. He limped towards me desperately, weaving, his head lolling. Each step seemed a strenuous effort and only courage forced him to take them.

'What have they done to you, boy?' I whispered, feeling my throat grow tight and tears begin to prick the back of my eyes. I didn't let them show. Crying wouldn't help.

Mylor stopped and managed the faintest of whinnies. I didn't realise it was meant as a warning. For a brief moment I saw the reflection of a gloved hand holding a torch in the shiny surface of his eyes – and then I felt the blow. It was as if a bull had hit me between the shoulders.

Glass broke and a tiny green feather fluttered through the air. It brushed my cheek as I dropped dizzily on to the black and white tiles. Somehow the feather seemed important and I can remember clutching it in my palm just before everything blurred. My head swam with noise – Spider barking, the scuffle of feet and a lot of jumbled remarks that didn't make any sense.

I lay where I'd fallen, not unconscious but too stunned to move. I suppose ten minutes must have ticked by before I heard a familiar voice. It was Angel.

'Roger's passed out, Professor! There's blood on the floor!'

Chapter Six

Waking up in bed was my next recollection. I opened my eyes and Angel's face came swimming into focus. She'd straddled a chair and was watching me closely, her chin resting on her arms. Professor Parkway stood at her side.

'Had a good rest, my boy? How are you feeling?'

I wasn't too sure. I thought about it for a while and decided that apart from a faint occasional throb at the back of my neck I could have been feeling a lot worse.

'You received a severe blow, Roger, yes indeed. Now I don't want you to worry about a thing, just try and relax.'

Bright sunshine was streaming in through my window. I was confused. 'What time is it?' I asked.

'Er ... twelve thirty.' He consulted his pocket watch. 'Almost lunch time.'

'Tuesday,' Angel added, pointedly.

'Tuesday?' I felt more dazed than ever. 'What happened to Monday?'

'You slept through it. The doctor gave you an injection and told us not to wake you.'

'Angel's been with you most of the time,' the Professor put in. 'Algernon and I have been extremely busy in the workshop.'

'Mylor?' I asked anxiously.

'Mending nicely, my boy. I think we were very lucky. The damage could have been much more extensive.'

'But his circuits –'

'A temporary setback, nothing irreparable. We're

having a few problems rewiring the electronic sensitiser but we'll overcome them, yes indeed.'

'In time for the Grand National?'

'Good gracious, yes. If we don't hit any more snags Mylor could be his old self in a couple of hours.'

That really surprised me. It made the intruders look amateurish – as if they'd bungled the job they'd set out to do. If their object had been to stop Mylor running in the National, then they'd failed because they hadn't been thorough enough. I knew they had enough skill to foil all the security devices, so why? It just didn't make sense.

'A penny for them.' Angel's eyes held mine.

'I was thinking about security,' I said. 'Boff was right, it does need improving.'

'I agree,' the Professor admitted. 'We appear not only to be dealing with ruthless people, but people with a great amount of technological know-how who gained entry with the aid of highly specialised equipment. The thumbprint button was countered by using an ultra-modern impulse jammer. Tch, tch, it's a sorry state of affairs when people have to stoop to such methods.'

'People like Doctor von Sternberg?'

'Now we mustn't jump to conclusions, Roger.'

'I have proof – or at least I did have.' I looked enquiringly at Angel. 'When I fell I was holding a feather. Did you find it?'

She nodded, hair swaying briefly across her eyes. 'I thought it might be important, so I've been keeping it safe.' She reached into the pocket of her snug fitting jeans and handed the little green plume to the Professor.

'Proof, Roger?' he queried.

'The Doctor wears a Tyrolean hat,' I explained. 'I remember the feather in the band very clearly – it's the same feather.'

'Zoot,' Angel murmured, 'so it is.'

The Professor knitted his brows. After a brief hesitation, he said, 'I admit it looks suspicious, but it's purely circumstantial.'

Angel gazed at him blankly, unsure of the word.

'It's not evidence, young lady,' he pointed out. 'To prove anything concrete against Doctor von Sternberg you'd have to produce the featherless hat.'

'Umph!' She plucked at her lip, then smiled suddenly. 'Roger and I could go –'

'Out of the question. Roger's not strong enough.'

'I do feel very weak,' I agreed.

'Of course you do. Only to be expected, yes indeed. You must stay with him, Angel, and nurse him back to health.'

Angel's eyes clouded. She nodded.

'See you both later,' the Professor did a backward shuffle to the door. 'Get plenty of rest, Roger, and you'll be up and about in no time.' He gave me a smooth rippling glance and departed.

Angel began fussing round me, straightening the covers and plumping my pillows. 'I hope you're not going to be a grumpy patient,' she began. 'If I've got to play nurse –'

'You haven't.' I threw back the eiderdown and swung my legs clear of the bed. I felt a trifle light-headed as I walked to the dressing-table. The reflection in the mirror showed a two-inch strip of plaster stuck to my forehead. 'What's this?' I asked.

'You fell on to some torch glass. It's not deep –' She stopped, put her hands on her hips. 'Roger, what on earth are you doing?'

'I'm getting up. We're going to the stables.'

She whirled. 'So all that stuff about you feeling weak was a lot of flummery.'

'I didn't want the Professor to worry. If he thinks I'm in bed then he won't.'

'You look very pale, Roger, are you sure—'

'I'm a little shaky, that's all. It's vital that I see Ought about Alaric's saddle.'

'Alaric's saddle?'

'I'll explain on the way. Load two bikes in the mazemobile and I'll meet you outside in five minutes.'

A quirk appeared at the corner of her mouth. She nodded enthusiastically.

'And don't make any noise,' I added. 'Be as silent as—'

'An Angel,' she said, wrinkling her nose.

I grinned as the door clicked shut.

Cycling from Parkway to the stables left me breathless. It was five miles of furious cross-country pedalling; a bumpy, bone-shaking ride that made me realise I'd been rather stupid in acting so hastily. My head was hammering and my pulse was racing as we circled the perimeter wall looking for a way in without being seen.

'There, Roger!' Angel braked hard and indicated a small door in the brickwork.

We rested our bikes against a tree and forged through a lot of spiky undergrowth to get to it. The latch was old and rusty and the frame nothing more than rotting wood pulp. Wherever it led, it was obvious that it hadn't been used in years. I got my fingers to the latch and pushed with all my weight. The bottom of the door scuffed the ground noisily as it brushed past a barrier of nettles.

We emerged by the side of the garage. Somebody was whistling and I could hear the sound of tap water filling a bucket. Edging carefully forward, I spotted a pair of patched jeans and scruffy shoes. Their wearer was bending over the bucket about to squeeze the contents of a car-wash sachet into the water.

'Isn't that...? Yes, it's Ought!' Angel burst out.

Her words made him jump. He swung round, his fingers closing on the sachet and sending a jet of green soap across the windscreen of Major Palmer's Bentley.

'Ooops!' Angel clapped a hand to her mouth. 'S-sorry,' she murmured inadequately.

He scowled. 'I should darn well hope so. Scaring the pants off people ought to be punished by six days of yard sweeping at least.'

'Let me help.' Angel took the sponge and sluiced the soapy liquid from the screen. 'There, no harm done.'

'No harm done! Car shampoos don't grow on trees you know. They cost ten pence each and Grogan'll skin me if he knows I've wasted it.'

'He doesn't have to know,' I said. 'There's still enough left if you eke it out.'

'It'll take a blasted lot of eking. This is a full-sized Bentley, not a Matchbox toy.'

'I didn't mean to scare you,' Angel apologised.

'Whenever you appear, I always end up spilling something. Last time it was the gruel, now it's –' He frowned suddenly and scratched his neck. 'What are you doing here anyway? What's Roger done to his forehead?'

I told him about the Parkway intruders and how I'd been knocked to the floor.

'If Spider hadn't woken us,' Angel added, 'Roger wouldn't have been found until the morning.'

'Did they nobble Mylor?' he asked.

'Nobble?'

'Get at him – harm him in some way so as to stop

him running in the National.'

'He's all right,' I put in quickly. 'Maybe I disturbed them in time or perhaps Doctor von Sternberg wasn't really trying.'

'Doctor von...? I don't understand.'

'It was the Doctor who hit me.'

'Grief!'

'I expect Rusty Grogan and Charlie Carver were there too. I heard several voices.'

'Grief!' he said again. He did a slow slouch round the Bentley, clicking his tongue and shaking his head. 'It all fits,' he murmured, more to himself than to us.

'What fits?'

'The conversation I overheard.'

'Well tell us.' Angel regarded him searchingly.

'I don't think I ought.'

'Why not?'

'I don't want to get involved – besides it's all very freaky. That Alaric isn't like a normal horse. I've never seen him eat anything and Grogan doesn't bother to muck out his box because there are never any droppings. It wouldn't surprise me if he was clockwork. Perhaps the Doctor winds his spring every morning with a whacking great key.'

'Have you seen it?' Angel's voice quickened.

'Seen what?'

'The key.'

'Course not,' he tut-tutted, adding, 'I was joking, you dope. Whoever heard of a clockwork horse.'

'It's not as funny as it seems,' Angel retaliated angrily. 'I could tell you things about Alaric that would make your hair – *Ouch!*' She let out a little cry as my shoe connected with her shin.

'Make my hair curl,' Ought finished the sentence looking suspicious. Hollows formed in his face as he squinted at me. 'You're holding something back,

99

aren't you?'

'Maybe,' I admitted, 'but so are you. Let's swop information. You tell me about the conversation you overheard and I'll tell you about Alaric.'

He looked unsure. He wiped his lips on his wrist and then his breath came gaspingly, forcing out the words: 'Y-yesterday, Rusty and Charlie were laughing their heads off. I heard them mention Mylor's name and say something about it being a good night's work. One less to worry about, Grogan said, and then Carver replied that you'd never find it in a million years.'

'Find what?'

'He didn't say. He just chuckled and said you'd know all about it at three fifteen.'

'Rats,' Angel huffed, 'I'd hardly call that information. How can you do a crossword puzzle with only half of the clues.'

'Three fifteen,' I mulled over the time. 'Today ... tomorrow ... when?'

He shrugged wearily. 'Wish I knew.'

My headache wasn't helping me to think. What he'd heard was a real brain-twister, but I was sure it linked up with what I already suspected – that the damage to Mylor's circuits was only a temporary measure, and that a far worse deed had been planned. I couldn't hope to guess what the 'it' was that we'd never find in a million years, so I simply asked him to keep his ears open and to let us know if he heard anything more positive.

'Okay,' he agreed, adding, 'Now keep our half of the bargain and tell me about Alaric.'

Angel was looking apprehensive. She was wondering just how I'd reply. I wasn't too sure myself, but eventually I said, 'He's a very special horse because he wears a magic saddle.'

'Magic saddle?' He stiffened, blinked. 'You must think I'm loopy.'

'Do you think Charlie Carver's loopy?'

'Carver?' His eyes grew thoughtful, curious.

'He's got three good saddles so why doesn't he use them? What would make him ride with a saddle supplied by Doctor von Sternberg?'

He scratched at the few odd bristles which sprouted on his chin. 'Aw hell, it's too much to swallow.'

'Suit yourself,' Angel said impatiently, 'but we're here to borrow it.'

'You'll be lucky. The Doctor keeps it locked away in his glittery travelling box.'

'Locked away?' I repeated. 'An *ordinary* saddle?'

He fell silent. His lips pursed and he hesitated before saying, 'Maybe there is something weird about it. The Doctor's always there whenever it's used.'

'So will you help us to borrow it?' Angel's voice was soft and excited.

'Don't you mean steal? If something's borrowed then it has to be lent – and you can bet your boots von Sternberg isn't going to do any lending.'

'We plan to return it,' I said. 'We're not thieves.'

'I want no part of it.' He turned his back on us and began fixing a hose to the nozzle of the tap. 'I ought to be getting on with my work. Now go away and I'll pretend I haven't seen you.'

Angel opened her mouth to say something but stopped as I shook my head. We left him to his car cleaning and set a determined course for the stable yard.

Lads seemed to be milling in all directions, tramping the concrete pathways which twisted round all sides of the yard in front of the loose boxes. Water buckets rattled and doors slammed as they checked their allotted horses. Brooms flicked away the odd wisp of straw in the final tidying-up process before lunch. Everybody was so busy that our presence seemed to go unnoticed. We headed for the parking area.

'There, Roger!' Angel indicated the Doctor's travelling box sandwiched between a tatty looking Mini and a Ford Transit van. The carnival lettering shimmered with dazzling brilliance as it was caught by the sun.

We kept low and by using parked cars as shields crept as near as we dared. The cab door was open and I could see Doctor von Sternberg's patent leather shoes dangling over the sill. A smoke ring appeared, then another, and then I caught a glimpse of a flat cap and a shock of red hair.

'Saddle's working fine, Doc,' Grogan's voice wafted towards us. 'Charlie ain't quite got the 'ang of the stirrups, but 'e reckons he'll be all right on the day.'

'He *must* be all right on ze day,' von Sternberg blustered. 'It is vital zat my Alaric wins ze Grand National. *Vital*, do you understand!'

'Okay, keep your hair on – nothin's gonna go wrong.'

'My hair? What has my hair to do with ze stirrups?'

'Nothin'. I –'

'You confuse me, Herr Grogan. First you talk about stirrups and then you talk about hair. I not know whether I am going or coming.'

'You mean coming or going.'

'I know what I mean!' He swore softly in German, adding, 'Now begin at the starting. Why does Herr Carver find ze stirrups disagreeable?'

'The steering's no problem,' Grogan said. 'Pressure on the left stirrup and Alaric turns left, pressure on the right and 'e goes right. It's the jumps that worry 'im – the kicking down 'ard on both irons at the right moment. Charlie's frightened of an electronic failure. If Alaric don't jump then he'll plough right through the ruddy fence.'

'Electronic failure!' The Doctor's voice was strained. I heard the rattle of girth buckles and an impatient slap of a hand against leather. 'I'm a genius with electronics! Zis saddle is a twentieth-century masterpiece. It has a fail-safe system and nothing – I repeat, nothing can go wrong!'

Angel leaned forward to almost the point of imbalance. 'He's holding it, Roger,' she whispered feverishly.

I grabbed the waistband of her denims. 'Come back here or we'll both be seen.'

'But he's got –'

'The saddle, yes I know. What we need is a plan.'

Her eyes flashed briefly. 'Couldn't we just dash out and grab it?'

'We could, only they'd probably grab us first. A diversion would be better.'

'Distract their attention you mean – like they do in films?'

'Well, something like that. I'll try to draw them away from the travelling box in the hope that the Doctor will leave the saddle in the cab. If he does then that leaves the coast clear for you.'

'I scoot out and snatch it?'

I nodded. 'Then we both run like mad for our bikes.'

She gave me a wisp of a smile and crossed her fingers.

I felt a little nervous as I eased from behind the cover of the cars and into the open. Gravel crunched under my feet and Grogan saw me almost immediately.

'It's that damn kid,' he said huskily as our eyes clashed.

Doctor von Sternberg almost fell out of the cab. He stared unbelievingly at me, clutching the saddle to his chest. A nerve in his face twitched.

'Hello,' I began, matter-of-factly. 'You're just the person I wanted to see.'

'M-me?' he croaked.

'Yes, I've made a special journey to return it.'

'*It?*'

'This.' I pulled the feather from my pocket and held it under his nose.

The corners of his moustache bunched. The feather fanned in my fingers as he let out his breath. 'Ich ... Ich verstehe Sie nicht,' he stammered.

Grogan frowned, shifting his cigarette from one side of his mouth to the other.

'The Doctor's telling me he doesn't understand,' I explained. 'Or do you speak German, Mr Grogan?'

'Don't get smart, kid!' Grogan flashed, punching a finger through a smoke ring. 'I ain't 'ad the benefit of your learnin', but I ain't no mug. Jus' what's your little game, eh?'

'I'm doing a good deed – returning lost property.'

'Does Major Palmer know you're 'ere?'

'Not yet.'

'Then beat it, you're trespassing.'

'Don't be hasty, Herr Grogan.' The Doctor blotted his forehead with a handkerchief, seemingly unable to take his eyes off the feather. 'Where exactly did you find...?'

'In the workshop at Parkway Grange. It must have fallen from your hat as you hit me.'

He gave an unpleasant grunt and did exactly what I'd hoped. The saddle was spread on the seat of the cab leaving his hands free to examine his hat. For a second or two he stood silent, studying the empty band thoughtfully. 'Ja,' he said finally, giving me his crocodile smile, 'I appear to have lost a feather and you appear to have found one. Similar, ja, but not ... how you say ... identical.'

'So you deny breaking into Parkway and clubbing me with a torch?'

'Course 'e denies it,' Grogan cut in, stepping forward. He smelled strongly of tobacco and sweaty socks. Twin spirals of smoke curled from his thin nostrils as he added scornfully, 'Now either you push off, kid, or I'm gonna personally throw you out!'

I deliberately backed up, drawing them away from the cab, putting at least two yards of ground between their heels and the saddle. If I could make Grogan angry enough – really give him cause to come at me – then Angel's chance of success would be pretty well guaranteed.

'I'm going to show this feather to the Major,' I threatened. I'll tell him how you hit me and about the damage you did to Mylor.'

Grogan's hard eyes glittered while he thought about that. 'Damage?' he queried.

'You smashed some of his circuits. You took a hacksaw to his electronic sensitiser.'

'Electronic...? Well, well, you do surprise me. Are you sayin' 'e ain't a real 'orse?'

'You know darn well he isn't. Neither is Alaric.'

Grogan dropped the cigarette, grinding it into the gravel with his heel. He gave me a penetrating look and said thickly, 'You're smart, real smart. So don't give me a lot of silly talk about blabbing to Major Palmer.'

'I mean it,' I muttered, laying it on. 'I'll tell him everything I know about Alaric and he'll report you to the Jockey Club.'

'Du dummer Junge,' the Doctor said in a constricted voice. 'Zat way nobody would benefit. All ze horses would be checked and ze inventors disqualified – including Professor Parkway.'

'A stalemate,' I agreed. 'You'd all have to wait another ten years.'

'*Mein Gott!*' He shook a fist at the heavens. 'You would not do this!'

'I would,' I bluffed.

Grogan was beginning to boil. 'Give me that feather,' he growled.

'Go jump in the lake.'

'Give me that –'

He lunged for my wrist but I side-stepped. He lost his balance and his temper as I hooked my foot around his ankle and sent him sprawling to the gravel. I saw his lips curl upward as he swore viciously, ordering the Doctor to 'get me'.

'I've got it, Roger!' Angel's voice speared the air.

'*Run!*' I shouted, wincing as von Sternberg's fingers dug claw-like into my shoulder.

I wriggled and managed to bring the toe of my shoe up hard against his knee-cap. He squealed and released. His eyes were wild as he went hopping away. I thought he was going to burst a blood vessel as he suddenly realised that Angel had taken possession of his saddle.

'Sie haben meinen Sattel gestohlen!' he yelled, helping Grogan to his feet.

We fled like two scalded cats. Out of the car park and into the stable yard, our legs pumping furiously, our hearts nearly bursting through our chests. Stable lads watched in amazement as we sprinted over the cobbles. A rider had just dismounted from a big bay horse and was in the process of loosening the girths. Our sudden appearance startled the animal and it shied across our path. I managed to veer round it but Angel wasn't so lucky. She stumbled and landed heavily on her knees.

'Are you hurt?' I took hold of her arm.

'I'll be all right.' She glanced wildly round, trying to recover her senses. 'They're getting close, Roger. We're ... we're going to be caught.'

'No we're not,' I gasped, dragging her on.

We bypassed the horse and dodged nimbly round a stable lad who was pushing a wheelbarrow. Angel clasped the saddle to her breast as if her life depended on it. The leathers flapped and the irons jangled with every hurried step. I could also hear a lot of panting and wheezing as the Doctor and Grogan followed in our tracks.

'*Halten Sie sie ein!*' The exclamation was close. Twenty yards, maybe less.

I risked a glance over my shoulder. The Doctor was still in pursuit but Grogan had stopped by the horse. He pushed the rider to one side, wrenched himself into the saddle and gathered the reins. Balanced and collected he yelled something like 'giddup!' and slammed his heels into the animal's flanks. The horse plunged towards us, its tongue writhing under the bit.

'This way!' I yanked Angel to the left and we angled across the courtyard to the garages.

'Blimey, what the...?' Ought gulped as he saw us. He was hosing down the Bentley and the nozzle went limp in his hands.

'T-turn it on Grogan,' I struggled to get my breath. 'He – he's following us on horseback.'

'I daren't. He'll kill me.'

'Not if your hand slips,' I suggested. 'You know – accidentally on purpose.'

'*Please*, Ought,' Angel said anxiously.

The thunderous chatter of hooves sent us bolting for the door in the brick-work. Above the din I could just hear the whoosh of increased water pressure as Ought turned the valve fully open. Droplets fell like rain as they bounced off the garage roof.

'You stupid...!' Grogan's voice broke into a gurgle as the stinging jet of water surged over his body and face. His cap went flying and he was very nearly unseated as his horse skittered away.

We fled for our bikes. I humped the saddle over my handlebars and got my feet to the pedals. Angel was already underway. Her legs worked furiously as she set a course for the fairly flat, shrub strewn area which lay to the west of the stables. As Parkway Grange lay to the east I suspected that Angel was gambling on Grogan taking the wrong route. I only hoped she was right.

A lot of swearing and shouting still echoed from the yard. Grogan was obviously very wet and blazing mad. He'd have to dismount, lead his horse through the gate and then remount. All this would take time and with luck allow us to get a long way clear and out of sight.

I did plenty of wobbling in my effort to gather speed. The saddle was cumbersome and made the bike difficult to steer. My sister was whizzing ahead, her fair hair streaming over her shoulders as she pedalled faster and faster. I knew I wouldn't catch her up but I was frightened of losing her. Five minutes must have passed and my legs were beginning to tire. Angel was now just a dot on the horizon but thankfully she'd stopped for a breather. I pushed on doggedly, over the rocky soil and towards a small clearing. I was light-headed with fatigue and this didn't help my bike tyres to avoid the stump of a broken post which suddenly appeared in my path. The front wheel hit it

The saddle was cumbersome and made the bike difficult to steer.
Suddenly the stump of a broken post appeared in my path ...

with a thud and Alaric's saddle went spinning from the handlebars. I lost my balance, the bike tipped, and I skinned my elbow on the way to the ground.

I lay limp, recovering my senses. My cheek was resting on a piece of warped plywood – some sort of notice board which had once belonged to the broken post. As I climbed giddily to my feet, the board's weather-beaten lettering swam before my eyes. It ran: OLD TIN MINE WORKINGS 100 YARDS AHEAD. DANGER UNSAFE GROUND.

I felt every one of the hairs on my neck rising individually as I looked towards Angel. I could just make out the ragged shape of some barbed wire fencing which had long ago acted as a barrier before being flattened by the wind. A tower with two large pulley wheels mounted at the top of the structure was also visible. Everything was in a state of disrepair, crumbling and thick with rust.

'The saddle!' Angel was shouting. 'Roger, the saddle!'

'Keep still!' My hands were shaking as I cupped them to my mouth. 'You're in danger. The ground's liable to give way!'

'What?'

'I said the ground's...' I stopped as I realised the wind was blowing directly in my face. I could burst my lungs and she still wouldn't hear me.

'Grogan!' Angel yelled, stamping her feet and pointing a finger. 'He's behind you, Roger. He's going to get –'

I turned as I heard the thud of hooves. Rusty Grogan swept past me riding circus style. He flashed me a surly glance as his hand whisked Alaric's saddle from the ground. He righted himself, laughed and held the saddle triumphantly in the air.

'Zoot!' Angel cursed, getting astride her bike.

I signalled frantically for her to stay put.

'You can't outsmart Rusty,' Grogan barked.

I swung to him. 'My sister...' I began, but he'd already turned and was heading at breakneck speed for the stables.

An earth-shuddering rumble dragged my eyes back to the mine. Panic bubbled up in me as the ground separated and a mountain of dust enveloped Angel. One second she was there with her bike, the next second she was gone. I heard a thin wail of a scream as the tower shook and the dust settled. Then only silence.

Chapter Seven

It's not easy to think when your brain's whirring and everything that has happened just seems like a dream. It's not every day that you find yourself in the middle of nowhere digging at soil with your bare hands because the ground has just opened and swallowed up your sister. It's not surprising that when somebody taps you on the shoulder to ask if they can help that you begin to think you're hearing voices.

'Roger ... Roger ... it's me, Ought.'

'Ought?' The name registered distantly. I turned round, dazed.

'What's happened? Where's Angel?' he asked.

'How ...?'

'When Grogan returned with the saddle I guessed you'd hit trouble. I thought I ought to take a look so I followed the tracks – hey, never mind about all that, where's your sister?'

'Buried.' My voice was unsteady. 'Sh-she's buried alive.'

'Holy cow!'

'The soil just gave way. She's under here. You've got to help me dig her out.'

He shook his head. 'This area's unsafe. If you disturb the ground then the whole lot's liable to collapse.'

'So what do I do,' I snapped, 'let her suffocate?'

'There's plenty of air down there. She's probably dropped to the tinstone layer. She might be hurt, but she'll be able to breathe.'

'You know the mine?'

'Everybody in West Devon knows it – or knows to avoid it. The tinners abandoned it years ago. Angel ought never –'

'Well, she did,' I cut in, 'and who can blame her. We're not local, we're from London – and there they put up protective barriers and flashing lights to indicate danger.'

'There was a sign ...' he began.

'A *broken* sign,' I corrected, 'and a fat lot of use that was. I only saw it because it punctured my front tyre.'

'Well ...' He chewed on his lip and his eyes went past me to the tower. 'We're going to need some heavy lifting gear and a lot of help to get her up.'

I followed his gaze. 'But that's the shaft,' I said. 'That's all of twenty yards from where she fell.'

He made an exclamation of irritation and led me to the tower. We stood under the huge rusty pulley wheels, our eyes tracing the cables which disappeared into the seemingly bottomless blackness. Ought tossed a pebble down the shaft. Three seconds later it struck something with a clang.

'That's the cage,' he informed me. 'It's about sixty feet down.'

'What of it?' I frowned.

'There's a rabbit warren of openings down there. All of them lead to the cage.'

I was beginning to understand. 'So if Angel can crawl to it then all we've got to do is haul her up.'

'Only the hauling isn't going to be that simple. This headgear hasn't been used for fifty years. The steel rope looks sound enough but we ought to have a crane at least if we're going to stand any chance of raising the cage.'

My eyes flitted over the dilapidated machinery. I could see the ramshackle steam winding engine, its wheels and pistons covered in moss; its once rotating drum now brown and pitted where the years had eaten it away. Ought was right, it wasn't going to be simple. The idea of a crane – the weight, the vibration sent shivers down my spine. With the ground so unsafe the shaft could well become a tomb.

'Look at the cable!' Ought's mouth fell open. Flakes of rust danced past his eyes as the steel stretched and creaked. 'It must be Angel, Roger. She's found her way to the cage!'

I swallowed and managed a grin. A hollow tapping sound echoed up the shaft. I listened carefully: *dot dot dot, dash dash dash, dot dot dot.*

'What's she doing?' Ought looked confused.

I rummaged in the soil for a piece of stone. 'She could be badly hurt,' I said. 'That's SOS in Morse.'

'Morse what?'

'Morse code, you chump. Angel and I learned it at school.'

'Never liked school,' he confessed. 'Never liked the teachers but I suppose I ought to have stuck it.'

I reached for the cable and replied by striking it with the stone. A series of long and shorts spelled out: We'll get help. Are you in immediate danger?

There was a long pause, then: *dot dash dash, dot dash, dash, dot, dot dash dot.*

'What's she saying?' Ought's forehead creased.

'Water,' my head pounded with the effort to think clearly. 'Angel's asking for water.'

'Asking for it, or telling you she's trapped in it?'

Fear cramped my stomach. I stared at him.

'She's sixty feet down, Roger,' he added tight-lipped. 'The tinners cut a trench at the lowest part of the valley to carry off the water but that's long since been blocked.'

'Jeepers! You mean she could drown?'

'Well ... er ...' He looked as if he could have bitten off his tongue. He tried to smile but it didn't work. 'Don't worry, Roger ... with the dry spell of late ...'

'But she could be up to her neck in water!'

'She could,' he gulped, 'but there's no point in panicking. Look, you stay here and I'll go for help. There's a breakdown garage in Swanfield and they have cranes and winches and things –'

'They'll bring the whole mine crashing down on top of her.'

'It's risky I know, but we haven't any other choice.'

'How about a horse?"

'Stardust?' He glanced at the old grey mare that had carried him faithfully from the stables to the mine. The horse chewed contentedly at a nearby fringe of grass. 'You think she could raise the cage – an old hack who's long past her best? Aw, c'mon Roger, you'd need a team of shire horses –'

'We need Mylor,' I said.

'Eh?'

'Mylor,' I repeated. 'Ride to Parkway, tell the Professor what's happened and bring him and the horse back here.'

He stared at me, blinked his brown eyes. 'Look. I know your horse is strong. I had to repair the box door he busted, but that cage weighs ... well, crikey, I don't know how many tons. No racehorse on earth can –'

'Mylor can,' I asserted.

'You're bonkers.'

'He's the most powerful horse in the world.'

'Round the twist. Daft as a brush. Plain blind blasted stupid.'

'And you're wasting time.' I began to walk towards Stardust. 'If you won't go then I will. I thought I should stay because I read Morse but –' I stopped as a sudden burst of dots and dashes vibrated along the cable.

I looked at Ought. 'Do you know what Angel's saying?'

'No.'

'She's asking us to hurry. She wants us to bring Mylor.'

The first part was true, the second part I invented. I knew Mylor had the strength to raise the cage but I knew it would take a request from Angel to convince Ought.

'Okay,' he lifted and dropped his bony shoulders. 'I think you both ought to have your heads examined, but I'll go.'

I gave him brief instructions about Parkway's security system and explained how he'd have to wait inside the gates until the Professor spotted him on the closed-circuit TV.

'I'll be back in forty minutes.' He hooked his left foot in the stirrup iron and sprang into the saddle. 'While I'm gone you'd better start thinking of a way to attach your miracle horse to the pulleys. It's not going to be easy.'

The reins made a fearful crack as he flicked them against Stardust's neck. The old mare bolted forward as if she'd just left the racecourse starting stalls. I tore my eyes away from the fast disappearing hindquarters and hurried back to the shaft.

I climbed the tower's rickety wooden steps and inspected the pulley wheels at close quarters. They were like something from a giant locomotive; spokes as thick as my arm with a massive iron spindle running through their centre. Once brightly polished and greased, they were now coffee-coloured and fossilised. They'd have to turn to lift the cage. I retraced my steps, coldly aware that perhaps I was asking just a little too much of Mylor's solar strength.

My feet trampled over various relics at the base of the headframe; heavy oak props, chains, some railway track, even a Davy lamp that had long ago been forgotten. I stood looking at the old winding engine. It was in a far worse condition than the pulley wheels, but perhaps I could turn that to my advantage. Fifty years of Devonshire weather had practically welded the cable to the drum and nothing on earth was going to make it rotate.

Sorting through the chains, I dragged out the heaviest, strongest and longest one I could find. I judged it to be about thirty feet in length with a hook at one end and a coupling at the other. It was perfect for what I had in mind.

I yanked it, lifted it and twisted it until I was exhausted and my T-shirt was sticking clammily to my body. The chain was now looped around the pulley cable, its two ends extending some fifteen feet beyond the drum and engine. My plan was simple, but it depended on three things: the pulley wheel had to turn to lift the cage, and the drum had to remain seized up to take the strain. As for number three, well that was up to Mylor and me. The chain would be coupled around his chest and he'd have to walk sixty feet (the depth of the cage) doing the job of the steam winding engine. The pressure would be colossal. I only hoped Mylor's toughened steel framework could cope with the load.

Some twenty minutes had passed since I'd last heard from Angel. I was beginning to worry. I laid the chains out neatly and crossed to the shaft. My Morse enquiry brought the reply: I'm cold, Roger. Please hurry.

I tapped back that Mylor was on his way and that

she'd be up in no time at all. I wasn't being completely honest, but I knew it was important to keep her spirits high. Thank goodness she couldn't see my crossed fingers.

Mylor's hooves were just a blur as they hammered across the open ground. The sizzling pace churned the soil into peaks and caused Professor Parkway to hang grimly on to the saddle. The ride seemed to be proving a painful experience and from the expression on his face I doubted whether he'd ever been on a horse before.

'I'm too old for this sort of activity,' he wheezed as Boff operated the dead-stop mechanism. He grabbed Mylor's mane and slipped in an ungainly fashion to the ground. His eyes were pouched and bloodshot. 'It's most uncivilised, Roger,' he added. 'I didn't even have time to make a flask of tea.'

'Angel's trapped underground,' I stressed, releasing the girths.

'You were supposed to stay in bed, not go gallivanting off to the stables.'

'We tried to get Alaric's saddle.'

'A very silly escapade.'

'I'm sorry,' I said weakly.

'I should hope so, yes indeed.' He threw a note of urgency into his voice. 'Now climb into the chest-hatch before that stable lad sees you.'

Ought was still a long way off and Stardust appeared to be labouring. It only took me a few seconds to outline my 'hoist' plan to the Professor and then I was up the treads and beside Boff in one bound, closing the chest-hatch behind me.

'Heck Roger, you really caught Gramps and me on the hop,' Boff breathed softly, settling himself into the second seat. 'We'd only just finished rewiring the electronic sensitiser when Ought arrived.'

'Are all systems functioning normally?' I ran my eyes over the dials.

'Better than ever.'

'Solar-storage?'

'Fully charged when we left.'

The journey had dropped the energy level by a third. That meant we could afford to expend another third in the rescue operation and still have enough power to get home. I backed Mylor towards the old winding engine and flicked the scan-switch. Stardust had just arrived and Ought was looking puffed.

'Your horse is faster than a streak of lightning, Professor,' he panted, finger-combing sweat-dampened hair from his eyes. 'A real flyer –' He stopped, squinted. 'Hey, where's Roger?'

The Professor cleared his throat nervously. 'Haven't seen him, my boy. We'll just have to manage on our own.'

'But aren't you worried, sir?'

'Roger can take care of himself. Let's worry about Angel for the time being.'

There was a thoughtful silence, then Ought muttered, 'I was telling him how the tinners had cut a trench at the lowest part of the valley – a sort of drainage system. I suppose he could be trying to unblock it.'

'Of course.' The Professor looked relieved. 'The trench. That's where he'll be. Roger's very industrious, yes indeed.'

'Phew!' Boff's breath hissed against my neck. 'I wondered how Gramps was going to explain your absence.'

'He really didn't have to,' I said. 'Ought put the words into his mouth.'

Boff grinned but his expression dissolved to one of

seriousness as the rattle of chains filtered from the dash speaker.

'Wrap Mylor's saddle around his chest,' the Professor was saying. 'We'll use it as a sort of cushion to stop the heavy linkage from chafing his skin.'

'This isn't going to work, Professor,' Ought said.

'Of course it is, my boy. I can't fault the principle. As Mylor pulls, so the chain draws the cable which turns the pulley wheel which—'

'The principle might be okay,' Ought interrupted, 'but no horse on earth can match the strength of a crane.'

'We'll see, we'll see. No time to waste talking. Is the saddle in position?'

'Y-yes, sir.'

'Then attach the hook to the coupling.'

The video screen showed Ought standing before us holding the chains in each hand. He mated the two ends then began clicking his tongue as a signal for Mylor to walk forward. I engaged the pace-selector and very gingerly opened the throttle. The metal links slapped against Mylor's flanks and quarters as I eased him into the crudely made harness. The slack was taken up. His chest began to take the strain.

'Whoa!' Ought ordered, ducking down to adjust the saddle. The pommel was pushed a little nearer to our horse's throat, while the sweat flaps were wrapped protectively around his shoulders. 'That's the best I can do, Professor,' he added. 'It's hardly armour-plating but maybe it'll stop his skin from being torn like tissue paper.'

'Well done, my boy. Now stand clear and watch those pulley wheels. Your eyesight is better than mine and I want to know the moment they move.'

He nodded and stepped away.

The Professor leaned towards the ear-mikes and

whispered, 'All right, Roger, it's up to you. Increase Mylor's power very gradually – no sudden jerks or you're liable to snap a cable. Keep calm. Good luck.'

I inched the throttle forward, increasing the pressure of the hydraulic fluid in Mylor's plastic veins. Five hundred pounds ... eight hundred ... one thousand ... My eyes never left the gauge. The cockpit began to vibrate under the strain. The chains groaned alarmingly as the power surged into the leg muscles.

'Nothing's happening,' Boff whispered raggedly. 'We haven't budged a blasted centimetre.'

'We're at half throttle,' I announced, 'but I'll have to accelerate still further.'

'Could be risky.'

'We'll have to chance it.'

I eased the lever towards the three-quarter marker. The ground beneath Mylor's hooves seemed to tremor like a minor earthquake. I could hear the chains searing into the saddle leather. The cockpit interior lights flickered crazily.

Boff squirmed in his seat. 'N-no more,' he blurted. 'You'll overload the circuits. We'll blow a fuse.'

'Angel's sixty feet underground,' I retorted. 'I've got to get her up.'

'Not at the expense of Mylor. There must be another way –'

'There isn't time. If we don't get her up, she'll drown.'

'But you'll break him, Roger! The stress is too great. Any more power and you'll drain Mylor's body far beyond the point of collapse!'

I wasn't sure which was shaking more, my right hand or the throttle control. I pushed it all the way forward, fully aware of the consequences, knowing I was driving Mylor to the limits but prepared to

The ground beneath Mylor's hooves seemed to tremor like a minor earthquake. I could hear the chains searing into the saddle leather as he pulled, taking one powerful stride at a time.

gamble that the cage would lift before electronic failure befell the horse.

'*Roger, no!*' Boff grabbed my shoulders, looked at me pleadingly.

The cockpit lights blinked, then went out. The video quickly followed suit.

'That's torn it,' Boff gulped. 'You've overtaxed the whole system.'

The luminous needles of the gauges danced before my eyes, little smudges of light in the darkness. The energy indicator had swung into the red 'danger' zone. I slowly realised that the cockpit vibrations had lessened. Wearily my brain told me we were moving.

'The pulley wheel's turning, Professor!' Ought's astonished voice blasted the ear-mikes. At least they were working. 'What a horse! What an incredible, unbelievable horse!'

'Mylor's done it,' Boff's breath escaped in a sigh of thankfulness.

'We're not out of the woods yet,' I said. 'Can you fix those fuses?'

'You bet.' He groped under the seat, snapped on a torch. 'Just give me a jiffy.'

Mylor pulled, taking one powerful stride at a time. I could hear the rhythmic creak of the wheel as it turned, paused, then turned again. It sounded sweet to my ears. Each revolution was bringing Angel that much closer to the surface. I relaxed a little, gently easing my grip on the throttle. The needle hung just outside the red zone.

Still no lights. 'Having problems?' I asked, looking over my shoulder.

'There's something odd here, Roger,' Boff murmured, concentrating the torch beam on one of the many equipment cover hatches. 'This inspection plate has been put on upside down.'

'Perhaps the Professor –'

'Gramps is too methodical.' He passed a hand over his hair in bewilderment. 'So am I. Neither of us would make that kind of mistake.'

'What does the plate cover do?'

'It's there for the fuses but you can also gain access to the solar generator.'

'Has that been giving any trouble?'

'None. It's working better than ever.'

I shrugged, not knowing what to think. The distance-indicator showed that Mylor had paced forty feet. Another twenty and Angel would be home and dry. I desperately needed the help of the video screen.

'C'mon, Boff,' I chided. 'We're running out of time.'

'Nearly ready, I've just…' There was a lot of snapping and clicking. 'That's got it – all in.'

The video brightened. The cabin lights gave a couple of irregular flickers then stayed on. Professor Parkway was walking in front of Mylor beckoning him forward. Ought was there too, his spiky hair almost standing on end.

'Easy now, easy.' He took hold of Mylor's bridle and glanced anxiously back to the tower. 'Angel can't be far short of the surface. We ought to be real careful or we'll overwind the cage.'

'Yes, indeed,' the Professor agreed. 'Go gently, Rog –' He coughed to cover his mistake. 'Er … Mylor. Very, very gently.'

I reduced power. My eyes were beginning to hurt with the sheer concentration of watching the distance-indicator. It was registering fifty-eight feet as Mylor took one more stride.

'I can see the top of the cage!' Ought's burst of excitement nearly fractured the ear-mikes.

The indicator notched up the final two feet. I

operated the dead-stop mechanism.

'She's there.' The Professor beamed his achievement. 'Mission accomplished.'

'Up safe and –' Ought paused, his face suddenly frozen, stricken. 'The chains, Professor! Look at...' The words faded in a babble of terror.

'What's happening?' I felt Boff's hands grip the back of my seat.

The cockpit shuddered violently. There was a terrifying screech of overstressed metal that set my teeth on edge. I tensed. My mind began to spin and I couldn't make any sense of my thoughts.

'Hell's bells!' Ought shrilled. 'The cage is slipping back. The chain links are spreading under the strain.'

'Help her out – quickly!' There was near-desperation in the Professor's voice. 'There's only a matter of seconds before...'

'Th-the links snap and the cage hurtles underground,' Boff stammered.

Ought disappeared from the video. His feet slapped hollowly over the soil as he streaked to the shaft. I fought down the panic that was rising in my stomach and scrambled to free the chest-hatch.

'What are you going to do?' Boff looked at me with grief-dulled eyes.

'I don't know,' I said, 'but I can't just sit here waiting for Angel to plunge to disaster.'

I didn't bother with the treads, I just jumped. I scooted through Mylor's hind legs and very nearly collided with the Professor. The close stuffiness of the cockpit had made me a little drowsy and I wasn't too sure of my bearings.

'There, Roger!' Professor Parkway, a tiny pulse hammering in his temple, indicated the tower.

What happened next was a mixture of blurred impressions – Ought on his knees extending his arms,

Angel's hands fluttering to be gripped, a glint of blonde hair, a shout – and then this deafening metallic twang as the links finally sheared.

The chain held so valiantly by Mylor whipped past our faces, snaking towards the pulley cable which snapped free, like an archer's bowstring. The wheel spun madly. A plume of dust erupted and covered the headgear. The cage descended with an earth-trembling rumble as it sped to the shaft bottom. I covered my ears and eyes with my arms. I couldn't bear to look or to think. Only a jarring crash beneath my feet told me the cage had reached the tinstone layer.

The Professor started to cough; loudly at first and then muffled by a handkerchief. Dust particles began settling in my hair. I lifted an eyelid and for a second I stood still, numb, bewildered. The shaft area was just a swirling mass of grit and rust. I walked slowly forward, screwing up my eyes, striving to pierce the powdery gloom. The breeze helped. Gradually the dust began to lift, and there silhouetted like ghosts in a brown fog...

'Angel! Ought!' I shouted the names hoarsely.

Professor Parkway arrived at my side. He stared speechlessly at the two figures, his mind too spent for either wonder or surprise.

'Yes, it's us,' Ought said, and hiccuped.

Angel bit her lip, fighting the after-shock that threatened to produce tears. Her hair was a bedraggled mess and she was soaked to the skin. The Professor struggled out of his old tweed jacket and wrapped it round her shoulders.

'You had us worried,' he said softly. 'Touch and go, young lady. Yes indeed.'

'Mylor s-saved my life, Professor. If it hadn't been for his strength...' She gazed at the horse, her eyes wide and startlingly blue.

Mylor turned to look at her. Boff must have switched him to instinct because he threw up his head and whinnied knowingly. Chain links and pieces of torn saddle littered his feet. I could see a fine line of bare steel running across his shoulder muscles. The constant chafing of the chains must have scored through the thermoplastic resin of his coat. At this distance Ought would probably put it down to a trick of the light, but I knew that if our secret was to remain a secret then I couldn't risk him getting any closer.

I said to Angel, 'Mylor's strength might have raised the cage but Ought's arms whisked you from the depths of that shaft.'

'I know.' Her voice was the barest murmur. 'I'm going to kiss them both. First Ought and then Mylor.'

Ought hesitated. 'Aw, Heck, that's really not necess –'

Angel stood on tiptoe and planted her lips on his. Ought winced a little and blushed. During the rescue he'd received a bruised cheek and a gorgeous black eye, but they didn't seem to be worrying him half as much as the kiss.

'There,' Angel said, linking her arm through the Professor's, 'now it's Mylor's turn.'

Ought looked relieved as they strolled towards the horse. 'You and your silly sister,' he murmured good-naturedly, wiping a sleeve over the red dust that clung to his brow and face. 'If ... if there was a prize for causing embarrassment, then you ought to get it.'

I grinned and guided him towards Stardust. The old mare was still chewing at a clump of grass and seemed completely unaware of everything that had happened. Ought removed the saddle and asked me to give it to the Professor.

'I can ride bareback to the stables,' he added. 'Can

Mylor manage three...?' He broke off, slapped his forehead with his palm. 'Of course he can – what am I saying. He's a Samson of a horse. You should have seen the way he pulled those chains. Boy, Roger, you don't know what you missed.'

'No,' I said, tongue in cheek. 'I bet it was quite a sight.'

His forehead creased. 'Where were you, anyway?'

'Er ... looking for the drainage trench.'

'I guessed as much. I told the Professor that's where you'd be.'

'Fancy that.'

'Mylor's terrific,' he enthused, leaping on Stardust's back and gathering the reins. 'A power-packed wizard of a horse – everything you said. When those chains began to stretch ... wow... It was incredible! It's a real shame you weren't around to see it.'

I agreed wholeheartedly and cursed my luck for being away. Inwardly, of course, I was smiling. If only he knew.

Chapter Eight

WE'VE GOT YORE DOG – SO STAY AWAY FROM THE
STABELS, ALARIC, AND THE SADDEL.
KEEP YORE PART OF THE BARGAIN AND HE'LL BE
RETURNED SAFE AFTER THE GRAND NATIONEL.
TELL ANYONE OR POKE YORE NOSES WHERE THEY
AINT WANTED AND HE'LL BE DUN IN.

'Zoot!' Patches of colour flared in Angel's pale cheeks as she snatched the crudely printed note from Spider's basket. 'Grogan's been here – he's kidnapped our cairn!'

Boff's face was bleak. 'Of all the nerve! While we were at the mine he must have ... What a filthy rotten trick.'

'Are you sure it's from Mr Grogan?' the Professor queried.

'It's from him all right,' Angel said bitterly. 'Look at the spelling. Anyone in primary school could do better than that.'

I peeled off my jacket and flung myself into a chair. With all the happenings of late, my mind was finding it difficult to keep pace. The Professor suggested tea and asked Boff to put the kettle on. Angel crumpled the note, sighed heavily, and said she'd prepare a meal when she'd changed her wet clothes.

'The boys will do the cooking,' the Professor announced swiftly. 'You're going to have a bath, young lady, and an early night. Roger can bring you a tray when you're tucked snugly in bed.'

'I won't sleep,' her eyes dwelt broodingly upon

Spider's basket. 'How can I when Spider's probably cold and hungry and missing us terribly. Grogan's an awful man. I know he'll ill-treat our dog – I just know it.'

'He's a swine,' Boff said with feeling. 'If I was older and bigger ... I'd ... I'd zonk him in the mouth.'

'Violence achieves nothing, Algernon,' the Professor put in.

'Boff wouldn't be able to see him anyway,' I remarked, trying to lighten the atmosphere. 'He'd have to take off his glasses, and without them he's as short-sighted as a dodo.'

Boff entered into the spirit of the joke by crossing his eyes and jumping around like a boxer. The knuckles of his right hand struck me playfully on the chin.

'Oh, stop clowning around!' Angel's expression became slightly sullen. 'Spider's been stolen and all you can do is play games.'

'There's no point in brooding,' I pointed out. 'We should have expected Grogan to take advantage of the house being empty. If anybody's to blame, then it's me.'

'You?'

'It was my idea we should go after Alaric's saddle. If I hadn't suggested it, you wouldn't have been trapped down a mine, and Boff and the Professor wouldn't have left Parkway.'

'You mustn't blame yourself entirely, Roger,' the Professor lit his pipe and regarded me through a cloud of smoke. 'The main gate siren has been inoperative since Sunday. Foolishly Algernon and I concentrated all our efforts on repairing Mylor and this left the security system sadly lacking.'

'We'll fix that siren after we've eaten,' Boff said. 'I've been working on a new design with new components 'which will make it completely vandal-proof.'

'That's known as locking the stable door after the horse has bolted,' Angel huffed.

'I'm afraid it is,' Boff agreed.

'And it isn't going to help Spider.'

Boff slowly shook his head and glanced anxiously at me.

'We'll get him back,' I said. 'We've outsmarted Grogan before. We can do it again.'

She brightened. 'Do you have a plan?'

'Not yet, but give me time.'

'Tomorrow, Roger – say we'll get him back tomorrow.'

'I can't promise –'

'But there's hope? An itsy-bitsy chance?'

'Sure there is.' I tried to look a lot more confident than I felt.

Her frown relaxed and she almost came close to smiling. She crossed the room and looked in the mirror. 'Golly, is this Angel Young or a scarecrow?'

'Could be either, yes indeed,' the Professor puffed smoke. 'Neither has the sense to know that standing around in wet clothes can lead to a chill.'

'Sorry,' Angel stopped prodding her hair and turned, 'it's just that if I'm left on my own then I'll mope. I'll think about Spider and be miserable.'

'So think about Mylor and be happy,' Boff suggested, transferring steaming water from the kettle to the teapot. 'He's stronger than I ever dreamed and he's going to win the greatest steeplechase in the world.'

'Are you sure? I – I mean really sure?'

'Of course I am. Aren't you?'

She pursed her lips. 'I suppose Alaric –'

'Hah!' Boff grimaced. 'He'll probably fall to pieces during the race. If he's so darned good then why is

Grogan doing his utmost to hamper us?'

Angel hesitated. 'We could have hampered *him* if we'd captured the saddle. We could have cut off the stirrup leathers before returning it.'

'Stirrup...?'

'Charlie Carver uses the irons to steer Alaric. The saddle controls the horses's every move.'

Boff fingered his nose thoughtfully. His eyes found the Professor's. 'Sounds like von Sternberg's using micro-pressure switches. What do you think, Gramps?'

'I don't want to think, my boy. Stealing saddles? Cutting stirrup leathers? Thoughts like that can only provoke more trouble, yes indeed.'

Boff fell silent. He filled four mugs with hot tea and handed one to Angel. 'Things will look a lot better in the morning,' he murmured unconvincingly.

There was a sudden glint of tears in Angel's eyes as she took a last lingering look at Spider's basket. She left her tea untouched on the sideboard and edged her way out of the room.

Professor Parkway sighed, gave himself two spoonfuls of sugar and then rather guiltily added a third. 'I hope, Roger,' he said, with a quick look of concern, 'I hope you weren't serious about trying to rescue Spider.'

'Well ... I ...'

'You were just trying to boost Angel's morale – am I right?'

'Er ... more or less,' I hedged.

'Good, good,' he wagged his head, obviously satisfied. 'Now let's get ourselves organised. Lots to do. Security to be attended to. Mylor's scuffed coat to be repaired.' He drained his mug of tea and squinted at his pocket-watch. 'Good lord, I haven't time to sit here chatting. I suggest you boys prepare the meal while I go to the workshop and mix up the thermo-plastic resin.'

Boff and I exchanged glances.

'Nothing too fussy,' the Professor continued moving sideways to the door. 'I'm sure you'll do your best. Something simple but nutritious.'

The door slammed shut.

Boff fiddled with his spectacles, and looked at a loss. 'How are you on omelettes, Roger?'

'Making or eating them?'

'Making.'

'I can rustle one up at a pinch.'

'Great.' He yanked open the fridge. 'Well rustle four up and I'll lend a hand.'

'How much of a hand?'

He grinned. 'By cracking the eggs, of course.'

I spent the whole of the following morning at the south field. It was the first chance I'd had to tackle the mock National fences and I found it an exhilarating experience. The controls came easily to hand and I suppose the knowledge I'd gleaned from piloting my father's light aircraft set me in good stead. Certainly Mylor sailed over them with effortless brilliance. Even the Chair – the biggest fence on earth – proved no more than a routine leap for our solar-powered horse.

I finished the practice session feeling pleased and pretty confident. I'd made a few errors on some of the landings, but they were only minor ones and I'd have them ironed out in time for the race. On Saturday, I told myself, we'd be perfect.

Paul arrived after lunch. He'd collected the Professor's racing colours from the seamstress in the village and the air was tense with excitement as he unwrapped the brown paper parcel.

'Gosh, aren't they super!' Angel gave a wide joyous grin and stroked the silks lovingly. 'Are they really your very own? I mean is the design ... er ...' she faltered.

'Exclusive?' I ventured.

'Yes, exclusive. Are they yours for ever and ever?'

'Of course,' Boff piped up. 'They're registered at Weatherby's in the Professor's name. Nobody can copy them – not now.'

'They remind me of the mazemobile,' Paul said as Angel held the shirt against his shoulders. 'Black spots on an orange background. I'll look like a huge lady-bird.'

'Then you'll fly away home – all the way to the winning post.'

Paul laughed.

Angel put on the silk cap and waltzed to the mirror. She was wearing her favourite faded jeans with embroidered back pockets and a vivid yellow blouse whose collar came up like buttercup petals under her chin. Paul's arrival had worked wonders in helping to take her mind off Spider.

'I'm going to be a lady jockey when I leave school,' she stated emphatically. 'I'm going to win all the big races and become famous the world over.'

'You'll have to serve your time,' Paul told her.

'Time?'

'Apprenticeship. A couple of years of hard work and long hours to qualify for your jockey's licence.'

'I'm not afraid of hard work,' she murmured mildly.

'Then you should have a word with Major Palmer. He knows you're a talented rider, so he might well take you on when you're older.'

Angel thought about that for a few seconds, then

shook her head doubtfully. 'I wouldn't work under Rusty Grogan,' she said. 'He's a hateful head lad and I'm never going to forgive him for –'

'Aren't we forgetting our manners?' the Professor broke in. 'Surely, Angel, you're going to offer Mr Steel some refreshment?'

She nodded listlessly. Talking about Grogan had turned her thoughts back to Spider.

'A coffee would be very welcome,' Paul said.

Angel stifled her emotions and smiled. She pulled the silk cap from her hair and crossed to the kitchen. Paul folded the racing colours neatly and handed them to Boff.

'Oh, rot!' Angel exclaimed. 'It's a new jar, Professor, and I can't unscrew the lid.'

'I think I'm needed, yes indeed,' the Professor excused himself and trundled away.

Paul looked uneasy. 'What did your sister mean, Roger, about never forgiving Grogan? I didn't quite catch –'

'The time he locked her in the tack-room,' I covered quickly. 'Angel isn't exactly in love with crusty Rusty.'

'He's gradually becoming more human,' Paul added conversationally. 'I think he's bought himself a dog, so he can't be all bad.'

Boff stiffened like a board. 'A d-dog,' he stammered. 'W-what sort of a dog?'

'I'm not sure. He was fondling it with Charlie Carver and I was some distance away. It began barking like blazes when he locked it in his van.'

'The Ford Transit van?' I probed.

He nodded. 'He'll have to get permission from the Major before he can keep it in his flat.'

Boff drummed the table with his fingers and looked at me steadily. I could guess what he was thinking, but for Spider's sake I knew I mustn't arouse Paul's suspicions.

'Is Grogan at the stables now?' I asked, trying to keep the anxiousness out of my voice.

'Sure.'

'And Charlie Carver?'

'No, he's left for Exeter races.'

A plan was beginning to form in my mind. I looked towards the kitchen, then whispered, 'Have you noticed that Angel isn't her usual bouncy self?'

'Mm, slightly subdued,' he admitted.

'That's because we forgot,' I said.

'Forgot?'

'Her birthday.'

'You mean that today is...'

I nodded gravely. 'Can you help us out?'

'How?'

'By giving us a lift to the stables. There are some shops nearby and we can get her a present.'

'Good idea. Can you get back okay?'

'We'll take a bus. No problem.'

Angel and the Professor returned with the coffee. Paul swallowed it in four quick gulps then looked pointedly at his watch. He said he had an owner to see and that it was time he was leaving. 'Congratulations, Angel,' he added, showing even white teeth in a slightly sheepish grin. 'Your special day, huh? Lucky girl.'

Her eyes darted to me and she opened her mouth to say something, but nothing came. I tried giving her a subtle signal to smile but this only confused her more.

Boff said quickly, 'Roger and I will see Paul to the main gate, Gramps. The mazemobile's been acting up a bit and I want to check it out.'

'Er ... yes, yes indeed.' The Professor rubbed his

chin, still pondering on Paul's words.

As we reached the door Paul gave Angel an admiring top-to-toe look.

'As you get older, you get prettier,' he beamed.

We hustled him outside.

Boff made two purchases from the paper shop near the stables – a box of stink bombs and a reel of sticky tape. When I asked him to explain why he needed them he merely produced his owlish grin and told me I'd find out soon enough. I didn't press him. He was the boffin of the team – the brains – and if he'd thought of an inventive way to rescue Spider, then that was fine by me.

We circled around the stables to the car park. The gates were threaded with a chain and heavily padlocked. I got a foot to one of the cross beams and hauled myself to the top. My baseball boots gripped the narrow shelf just long enough for me to catch a glimpse of Grogan's Ford van.

'Is it there?' Boff asked anxiously as I slipped back to the ground.

'It's there,' I said.

'Anyone about?'

'Not that I could see.'

His gaze wandered to the top of the gate. 'It's very high, Roger. I'm not sure whether –'

'You go over first,' I coaxed. 'That way I can give you a leg-up.'

He seemed undecided. At school he'd never been one for football or running and his idea of a game stretched no further than pocket chess in the lunch break. (He was so good he could even beat the teachers!)

I hooked my fingers into the belt of his corduroys and heaved him to the cross beam. He wobbled a bit and clung to the gate for grim death, but eventually he straddled the top and by the time I'd leapt up to join him he'd tumbled awkwardly over the other side.

He dusted himself down and wiped his glasses. 'Phew!' he breathed as I joined him, 'that's a heck of a long drop.'

'All of eight feet,' I agreed.

'And we'll have to climb back to make the 'phone call.'

'Huh?'

'My plan,' he smiled suddenly, secretively. 'How good are you at voice impersonations?'

'I've never really –'

'You'll be fine. Just put a handkerchief over the mouthpiece and talk deeply. Grogan will never guess it's you.'

'Grogan...?' I was lost, confused. 'Boff, what exactly are you going to do?'

He gave a quick glance and beckoned me to the Ford Transit. We scooted past von Sternberg's travelling horse-box and arrived seemingly unnoticed at the van.

'We've a fair chance,' he said, snapping open the driver's door. 'Unlocked, but no keys in the ignition.'

There was a steel bulkhead with a window between the cab and the rear compartment. We climbed in and pressed our noses against it. Spider cocked a beady eye at us and wagged his tail furiously. He was sitting in a makeshift basket – a large spare tyre half-covered with a blanket – and the rubber had blackened his coat making it streaky and thoroughly untidy.

Boff walked round to the rear door and rattled the handle. 'As I expected,' he murmured, 'it's well and truly locked.'

'Then we haven't a fair chance,' I said grimly. 'Without keys...'

He pulled the stink bombs and sticky tape from his pocket and grinned hugely.

'How will they help?' I asked.

He didn't answer, just chuckled to himself. Leaning into the cab, he proceeded to tape the three little glass capsules behind the van's brake pedal. I began to grin too. I still wasn't completely sure of his plan, but some of the pieces were coming together.

'Catching on, Roger?' he winked.

I pinched my nose and made a face. 'The capsules will smash as soon as Grogan puts his foot on the brakes.'

'And three bombs will make one hell of a pong. He won't be able to breathe. He'll leave the van quicker than you can say Bad Eggs.'

'It's a knockout practical joke, but how will it help Spider?'

'Practical joke!' he protested. 'It's nothing of the kind. It's a carefully constructed plan of action to unlock that back door.'

'I don't get it.'

'I'll make it clearer. If you were driving from here to Exeter, where would you first use your brakes?'

I mentally traced the route. 'At the Swanfield T-junction,' I said. 'A quarter of a mile down the road.'

'Precisely.' He nodded smugly.

'Precisely what?'

'Grogan will apply the brakes at that spot, the bombs will burst, and while he's floundering for air we'll grab the ignition keys and rescue Spider.'

'It's good, but what makes you so sure he'll be leaving for Exeter?'

'Your 'phone call.'

I looked at him blankly.

'There's a call-box by the T-junction,' he explained. 'You're going to ring Rusty Grogan and pretend you're a policeman.'

'I'm what!'

He cleared his throat, deepened his voice. 'Good afternoon, Mr Grogan, this is Sergeant Smithers of the Exeter Constabulary...'

'I can't say that.'

'Of course you can – you have to. It's a guaranteed way of getting Spider back.'

I glanced at our cairn. He'd curled himself into the hollow of the tyre and was peering at me with soulful eyes.

'Well?' Boff prompted, closing the driver's door.

'I'll do it,' I said.

'Knew you would,' there was an irritating note of humour in his voice. 'Let's head for the road. By the time we reach the call-box you'll be word perfect.'

We retraced our steps to the gates and Boff lost some of his confidence when he remembered how high they were. I had the distance measured, took a run at them and made the cross beam on the first jump. I pulled myself up until my chin was over and then hooked my leg around the top. In a moment I was sitting astride the gates, extending my hands, and calling for Boff to make his run.

He gritted his teeth and made a determined effort to copy me. He was completely unbalanced as he sprang for the cross beam and his black school shoes (not the best footwear for climbing) half skidded, half scrambled, as he reached desperately for my hands. I gripped his shirt, pulled him hard, and he did a sort of forward somersault on his way to the other side. Unbelievably, his glasses stayed on and he landed feet first. The only trouble was he didn't let go of *me*, and instead of the smooth drop I'd planned, I hit the ground with a force that stung my ankles right up to my hips.

'Wasn't too bad, after all,' he said shakily.

'No,' I replied, wincing as I walked. 'You could almost say you flew over.'

Six minutes later we arrived at the T-junction. Boff tutored me on the way, giving precise instructions on what I had to say to Grogan. I experimented with various voices and eventually decided that the best effect was obtained if I only spoke out of the corner of my mouth. I used a strip of the sticky tape to seal off a section of my lips and then I covered the telephone mouthpiece with a handkerchief.

Boff consulted his pocket-book and dialled the number. I heard the rapid pips and pressed in a coin. Major Palmer's voice echoed down the wire:

'Good afternoon, Swanfield Stables.'

'Er...' I hesitated as my stomach turned over. Boff dug me in the ribs and I plunged on, 'I – I'd like to speak to Rusty Grogan please.'

A pause, then, 'He's in the yard. Hold the line while I get him.'

The receiver clattered down on his desk. Several seconds passed and then I heard a door slam and the sound of approaching footsteps.

'Yeah?' a voice grated.

'Mr Grogan?'

'Speakin'.'

'Sergeant Smithers here, sir, of the Exeter Constabulary.'

'Police?'

'I believe you know a Mr Carver...' I paused deliberately as if reading the name. 'A Mr Charles Carver.'

'Charlie? Sure I know 'im. Why, what's 'appened?'

'I'm afraid he's had rather too much to drink, sir. He caused a rumpus at the races, so we're detaining him at the station.'

'Oh, Gawd!'

I wanted to grin but the sticky tape prevented it. 'We'd be grateful if you could come and collect him, Mr Grogan. I understand he's a jockey who's riding in Saturday's Grand National but he's saying some very peculiar things.'

'Th-things?' Grogan muttered feverishly.

'He's telling us to bet our wages on an electronic horse called Alaric. Something about a special saddle that's fitted with micro-switches. It's nonsense I'm sure, but if the newspapers get to hear –'

'Gawd!' he said again. 'It's the drink ... don't let 'im out of your sight ... I'll be right over.'

He banged the 'phone on to the rest. The dial tone buzzed in my ear.

'Well?' Boff raised questioning eyebrows.

I peeled the sticky tape from my mouth and smiled. 'Prepare for the pong,' I said. 'Operation Spider is underway.'

We fled to a nearby clump of bushes and buried ourselves in the heart of them. Boff felt in his pocket and produced a two-pence piece. He weighed it in his right hand, spun it upwards and caught it neatly on its descent. 'Heads or tails?' he asked, smacking it on the back of his left hand.

'Heads,' I said.

He uncovered the coin. 'Heads it is. Do you want to hamper Grogan or go for the keys and rescue Spider?'

I was about to say the keys and the rescue but then I remembered that Boff wore spectacles and wasn't really cut out for the part of hampering.

'I'll take care of Grogan, you get the dog.'

Boff nodded, breathed relief.

We waited, our eyes fixed unblinkingly upon the strip of road. The stillness was suddenly broken by the purr of an engine – a purr which developed into a roar as the Transit forged towards us.

'Strewth!' Boff exclaimed. 'He's coming a hell of a lick.'

The van was about a hundred yards from the T-junction and closing rapidly. He'd have to use his brakes soon, I told myself, watching the blur behind the windscreen take on the shape of a flat cap which harboured a hard face with a cigarette stuck in the corner of its mouth. There was a grating squeal as a lower gear was hurriedly selected. The engine screamed alarmingly.

'Now,' Boff urged, 'stop now!'

He did. I saw the red brake-lights flicker and stay on. I could almost hear the crunch of the stink bombs as they disintegrated beneath the pedal. Certainly I could see the effect as the cigarette fell from Grogan's lips and his face twisted in a ghastly grimace. The van weaved drunkenly as he grappled to open a window. It mounted the kerb, ploughed a rut in the grass verge, and grazed a tree trunk as it finally shuddered to a standstill.

'C'mon!' I dragged a mesmerised Boff from the cover of the bushes and we streaked towards the Transit.

Grogan staggered from the driver's door coughing and fighting for air. His eyes were streaming and he'd completely lost his sense of direction. He fell over the bonnet and lay there wheezing.

The smell was diabolical. A dozen skunks couldn't have done a better job. Boff pressed a handkerchief to his face and snatched the keys from the ignition. He'd have to be fast. The effects wouldn't last for ever and once Grogan's lungs cleared we could well find ourselves on the wrong end of his temper.

Boff spoke with a trace of panic. 'There are so many

keys, Roger. I don't know which one fits the rear door.'

I ran to help him. His fingers shook as each key refused to penetrate the lock.

'Here, let me,' I picked a well worn one clear of the bunch. It was a lucky guess. The handle turned.

Spider barked a welcome and leapt into Boff's arms. 'Hey ... Spi ... stop that ... don't be so darned...' Boff squirmed as the little dog saturated him with kisses. He took a couple of steps backwards, then froze in his tracks.

I followed his gaze. Grogan's piggy eyes were visible through the bulkhead window. He'd recovered his senses and his face was full of hate. He straightened his cap, tucking the coarse, matted hair that had fallen over his forehead under the brim. Slowly, very slowly, he ran a furry tongue over his lips and brought his fist down hard on to the Transit's bonnet.

'I'm gonna ring your ruddy necks,' he grated. 'You'll be like chickens in me 'ands.'

'Smile,' I said to Boff. 'Stay exactly where you are and smile.'

'W-what?' His breath came in a weak rasp.

'Don't move an inch.' I tossed the blanket away and pulled out the old rubber tyre which had served as Spider's bed.

As Grogan moved round the left hand side of the van, I crept round the right. Boff stood his ground, a crooked scared-to-death grin pinned to his mouth.

'So you think it's funny, eh?' Grogan's footsteps were rapid, assured. 'Havin' a good laugh at Rusty's expense?'

Ice ran down my shoulders to my fingertips. I reached the front of the Transit, drew three long breaths, and sprang from the bumper to the bonnet to the roof. I held the large tyre above my head in order to keep balance. The rubber soles of my baseball boots were noiseless as I motioned towards the rear.

'You've caused me a lotta trouble,' Grogan was saying. 'You're in my debt, kid – and I aim to collect!'

I could see his cap now, the shoulders and back of his grimy jacket, the creases in his shirt and trousers – like a well-slept-in pair of pyjamas.

He stopped suddenly, glanced round. 'Hey, where's that fair-haired...?'

Boff's eyes lifted. Grogan twigged and spun on his heel. I leapt from the roof like a spring uncoiling. The tyre was released mid-drop and it found its way over his head in the winning manner that a hoop encircles a fairground prize. I gave it a little help by landing my full weight on its rim. It jammed over his shoulders, pinning his arms to his side.

'You damn ... AAAAHHH!'

He banged against the van and rebounded. His pale face had turned red with rage and his jaw quivered with the tension. The tyre held him like a bear hug and as he wriggled to get free his feet tangled and he overbalanced. Boff watched open-mouthed as he bounced and rolled away from us. He slid down the verge and into some brambles.

'It'll take him hours to get free,' I said, 'but I think we'd better hang on to these just in case.' I pulled the keys from the lock and pocketed them.

'He was going to wring my neck,' Boff remarked, still looking shaken.

'He ended up ringing himself,' I grinned.

'Your cairn looks hungry.'

'We'll get the bus back to Parkway and give him a good feed.'

Spider barked his agreement and licked my ear.

145

The tyre was released mid-drop and it found its way over Grogan's head in the winning manner that a hoop encircles a fairground prize.

Chapter Nine

Things gradually slipped back to normal. Angel, of course, was delighted with Spider's return and immediately regained her bright, bubbly personality. Professor Parkway remained a little distant, obviously angry that we'd attempted the rescue. I think it was an act rather than real anger. He'd spent all day Thursday watching me take Mylor over the practice fences and although trying to keep a you-were-lucky-to-get-away-with-it look in his eyes, he'd ended up smiling and congratulating me on the horse's performance.

Friday was a day of rest. Mylor was put on solar-storage and allowed to soak up the sun until his batteries were nearly bursting. We just lazed around, enjoying the last moments of companionship and that lovely mixture of jolliness and cosiness. Our Easter holidays ended with the Grand National. On Sunday it was back home to London, and on Monday back to school.

The Professor had hired a travelling horse-box and driver from a neighbouring stud farm to take us on the long four-hundred-mile journey to Aintree. It meant an early start, and at two a.m. on the Saturday morning we were ushered from our beds, issued each with a sleeping bag and told to make ourselves comfortable with Mylor.

One thing I can tell you, bumping about in a travelling box for eleven hours isn't the best way to have sweet dreams. At eight o'clock we opened a flask of tea and ate Marmite sandwiches. Boff lay back with

fingers interlaced behind his head, yawned and remarked that Paul would shortly be leaving Swanfield
to join us. The jockey was flying to Aintree in a small
chartered 'plane. Lucky Paul.

Soon after midday we arrived at the course. Any
weariness we might have been feeling was quickly lost
in the general excitement and hubbub of the stable
area. The Professor had fully briefed us on what to
expect, so we all slipped into our respective roles with
the least amount of fuss.

Mylor was on manual and I was at the controls as
Angel led us down the ramp. Boff and the Professor
followed at our heels carrying a larger wicker basket
full of tack and grooming materials. The Professor
signed the stable register and a security guard
checked each identity card. We'd been allocated box
number two and the stable manager escorted us to it.

'Sorry about the view,' he apologised, indicating a
recently flattened area that was crammed with construction equipment. 'We're extending this end of
the racecourse stables to accommodate more loose-
boxes. It was supposed to have been finished last
week, but as you can see...' He shrugged, smiled.

'An ugly looking brute,' the Professor agreed, his
eyes straying to a bright yellow bulldozer which over-
shadowed us. Its mechanised shovel reached skywards,
like a huge clawed hand. 'Tch, tch. A purely func-
tional instrument of destruction. No sleekness, no
graceful lines.'

'Which can't be said for your entry ... er ...' he
consulted his clipboard. 'Mylor, from West Devon.
He's a giant – stylish, yet one of the biggest horses I've
ever seen.'

'Thank you,' Professor Parkway beamed with
pride.

'I see we have another runner from your neck of

the woods,' the stable manager went on. 'Alaric, box number one. Are they trained at the same yard?'

'No, they ain't,' Grogan's head popped over the door in answer to the question.

'Zoot!' Angel gasped. 'We're next to that hateful man!'

'Stone the crows,' Boff murmured.

Grogan stared at them with a smouldering anger. A different Grogan. A specially-spruced-up-for-the-Grand National-type Grogan. Red hair trimmed and plastered to his head, tie, stiff collar and an almost white shirt. Black pin-stripe suit, neat, apart from a shower of dandruff on the shoulders and one gold and one silver cufflink poking from the jacket arms. His nose looked different, too. I edged nearer to the video, grinning as I realised his face was swollen with bramble scratches.

'You can't disguise riff-raff,' Angel remarked, with intentional insolence. 'You look like a dummy in a charity shop window.'

'And you smell of cheap soap,' Boff added bravely.

Grogan grew two inches taller at a jerk. He pushed a cigarette between sneer-curled lips and was about to make a forceful reply, but the stable manager beat him to it:

'No smoking, Mr Grogan. Please observe the notices.'

'Yeah,' he smiled nastily. 'Sorry.'

Horses were arriving in droves. There was a terrific hullabaloo at the gate and someone's arrival was causing panic among the security guards. Cheering, hand-clapping and shrieks of laughter erupted as stable lads jostled one another in an effort to catch a glimpse of the trouble.

'What on earth . . .?' The stable manager's forehead creased. He excused himself and hastily departed.

Mylor's video eyes offered a height advantage over the bobbing heads. I flicked the scan-switch until the trouble spot centred on the screen. A big, burly man with bloodhound eyes and a flabby, freckled face was shaking his fists in the air. The cause of all the laughter was lying at his feet. It was a horse – or at least a reasonable imitation. Its front legs had splayed out at the shoulders, and in a series of grinding, creaking metallic crashes it had shuddered to the ground.

'Metal fatigue,' Grogan sniggered. 'I'm surprised 'e even managed to reach the course.'

'More of your dirty deeds, I suppose,' Angel said tightly.

'One of Charlie's,' Grogan admitted. 'Ain't it amazin' what damage you can do with a screwdriver and a chisel?'

'Beast! Cheat! You don't know the meaning of fair play!'

He leaned forward giving Angel a close-up view of his yellow teeth. 'I know how to win, kid,' he growled, 'and that's all that counts.'

'You're neither a sportsman nor a gentleman,' the Professor said, with a twitch of his bushy eyebrows. 'You've destroyed in a matter of seconds something that took ten years to build.'

'Yeah,' he smirked. 'One down, four to go, eh, Prof?'

'Beast!' Angel said again, throwing her arms protectively around Mylor. 'You try and touch one hair of our –'

'I won't go near 'im, kid.' He glanced at his watch, gave another brainless laugh and spat on the ground between them. 'For me own safety I'll be keepin' as far away as possible.'

The laugh grew harsher, as if he was enjoying a

private joke at our expense. He bolted Alaric's door and crossed the stable area to the gate. Racecourse officials had cleared away the crowd of onlookers and were now carrying out a detailed examination of the broken horse. The big man with the freckled face appeared to be weeping.

'Is that one of the inventors, Gramps?' Boff asked.

'Indeed it is, my boy. That's the Count de Chartres, a Master of Science and a thoroughly brilliant man.'

Boff pulled his racecard from his pocket and ran a finger down the list of entries. 'I've found him. His horse is called Noble Ransom.'

'*Was* called Noble Ransom,' the Professor corrected sadly. 'He's just scrap metal now and there's nothing very noble about that.'

Scrap metal? The words had a horrible ring to them. They started me thinking. Could that happen to Mylor? Could he end up as scrap? A useless piece of junk for someone to put in a melting pot and turn into hundreds of saucepans or thousands of stainless steel knives and forks. I remembered the night he tried to warn me – how guided by instinct he knew that I was a friend and von Sternberg an enemy. He could distinguish between good and evil and I didn't believe it was all due to transistors and printed circuits. I preferred to think that tucked away in all that electronic apparatus there was a tiny core of realness.

'Scrap, indeed!' I shouted the words, letting them echo round the cockpit.

Not *our* entry! Not Mylor! No, I reassured myself, that couldn't happen to the most powerful horse in the world.

'I think I can hear Roger shouting, Professor.' Angel's anxious voice leaked from the dash speaker.

'Indeed, young lady. He's probably hot and wants

to come out. Take Mylor right inside the box and I'll close the door.'

I tweaked the throttle just enough to move us forward. The video screen darkened as the split doors were slammed shut. I closed down all systems and opened the chest-hatch.

'Time marches on,' Angel said, above the hiss of the pneumatic dampener. 'I'll make a start on grooming Mylor. I want him to be the most beautiful horse in the parade ring.'

'Mmmm – sure,' I yawned, stretched and pressed the forelock button. Sunlight streamed in as Boff opened the top half of the box door.

'Take a look at this, Roger.' Boff handed me his racecard and brought my attention to the six ticks pencilled down the margin. Alaric, Mylor and Noble Ransom had been marked off, but the three remaining horses meant nothing to me.

'These are the special entries,' he explained on seeing my puzzled expression. 'Gramps recognises the owners' names, they're all inventors.'

'Do we know their box numbers?'

He slowly shook his head. 'Only what they're called, I'm afraid. Are you anxious to see them?'

'A peep wouldn't do any harm.'

'I suppose we could go from box to box, but with over forty runners –'

'*Can I have your attention, please!*' The stable manager's voice cut him off. He'd cupped his hands to his mouth and was addressing himself to the little knots of people who were gathered at each loose-box. He waited until he had absolute silence then continued. 'The clerk of the course has instructed me to carry out an inspection of the horses. This has become necessary because of the Count de Chartres' entry, Noble Ransom, collapsing on arrival. The Count's runner, as no doubt most of you saw, turned out to be nothing more than a very clever piece of machinery. It's quite possible that there are more of these "machines" masquerading as horses. We intend to find out. Please stay by your respective boxes until the check has been completed. Thank you.'

'Crumbs,' I murmured, 'this could be dodgy.'

'And it's all Grogan's fault,' Angel retorted tartly, banging a dandy brush hard against the box door.

'We've nothing to fear,' Boff spoke cheerfully enough, but for all that he looked rather pale. 'Mylor's perfect. If he's good enough to fool Paul then he's good enough to fool anyone.'

'Paul's never had cause to look for a forelock button or a chest-hatch join,' I reminded him.

The Professor, who'd been unpacking the tack, nodded and tapped his teeth thoughtfully, 'Roger's right, yes indeed. If we're not careful we could find ourselves disqualified.'

If the situation hadn't been such a serious one I might well have found it funny. The stable manager aided by a security man went from horse to horse poking, prodding, looking into mouths, and risking the odd playful nip or kick as his hands ran over the ticklish spots. Fifteen minutes passed and a dozen horses had beeen certified as genuine. They'd started at the high numbers and were working down to the low. Mylor and Alaric would be last. The waiting was going to be hell.

'Doin' a check, are they?' Grogan arrived back. He was grinning from ear to ear. 'This should be a good laugh. Jus' wait till they reach Golden Hope.'

Boff's eyes dropped to his racecard. 'That's Baron Glaster's entry,' he said. 'It should be a super machine. The Baron's a director of CAT.'

'CAT?' I queried.

'College of Advanced Technology. He'll take a lot of beating.'

'Not if he loses his nine lives,' Grogan sniggered. 'They've reached his box now. Somethin' tells me the 'orse ain't gonna be too cooperative.'

Golden Hope was backed out of his box for inspection. He was a nice looking sort, big and rangy, light bay in colour with three white coronets. The stable manager called a halt but the horse didn't stop. He just kept going backwards ... and backwards ... and backwards...

'Whoa!' the security man shouted. 'Hold up there! Hold up!'

Stable lads scattered as the horse continued his backward robot-like walk. We froze ... literally stiffened, our mouths hanging open as the animal's rump crashed sickeningly into an opposing wall. It shook a few bricks loose and then its mechanism shrilled harshly as it jammed. There was a loud twang like a broken piano string, and then it collapsed.

'Got stuck in reverse,' Grogan chuckled mockingly. 'Now I wonder 'ow that 'appened? What a shame. What a terrible, terrible shame.'

Angel whirled on him. 'You're not sorry! You knew it was going to happen because you made it happen!'

'Yeah,' he congratulated himself. 'Busy little bee, ain't I?'

Boff's eyes flashed to his racecard. 'W-what about Trace Element and Lexander?' he quavered. 'What swinish devilry have you done to them?'

'None. They ain't 'ere.'

'But they're listed –'

'I know they're listed, my little four-eyed friend – but they 'aven't arrived. Their horse-boxes broke down on the way to the racecourse. Tut, tut, can't rely on nothin' these days.'

The Professor's eyebrows came together in a fleeting scowl. 'Mr Grogan, you're despicable,' he grunted.

'Don't know what that means, Prof. I 'ope you ain't sayin' nasty things. I'm very sensitive. I don't like my feelings 'urt.'

'There isn't a strong enough word in the English language to describe my bitterness,' the Professor retaliated. His face was red and positively bulging. I'd never seen him so angry.

Grogan laughed. It was a throaty laugh that brought goose-pimples out on my flesh. 'Jus' Mylor and Alaric left,' he mused. 'Two out of six. The odds are gettin' better all the time.'

Twenty more minutes ticked away. A seemingly endless stream of horses passed through the stable manager's hands. Each was inspected closely before being given a nod of approval. Finally it was our turn.

'Mylor ... ah, yes, I remember,' the stable manager said pleasantly, consulting his clipboard. 'A big flashy chestnut from Devon.' He smiled at Angel. 'Bring him out, missie. Let's have a close-up look at him.'

Mylor emerged from his box looking as handsome as ever. He arched his powerful neck and viewed the two men through eyes that were bright and alert. Rather than have me inside, the Professor was putting his trust in Mylor's instinct circuits to carry him through the stickiest inspection he'd ever had to face.

'A fine piece of horseflesh,' the stable manager said admiringly, running his hand down the back tendons to the fetlock joint. He spoke quietly to Mylor and lifted the animal's forefoot. 'Mm, good, good. Nice neat heels. Who's been busy with the hoof-oil?'

'Angel does most of the grooming, sir,' Boff responded.

'Well done.'

Angel smiled prettily.

'Nothing amiss here,' the security man stated, probing Mylor's soft mouth. 'The teeth are all good – do you want me to count them?'

'Oh, tosh!' Angel broke in, her eyes flickering to the stable manager's long fingers as they strayed to stroke Mylor's forelock. 'How silly! There'll be forty or forty-two teeth just like any normal stallion.'

The stable manager looked surprised. His fingers stopped short of the forelock and he scratched the side of his nose instead. 'You obviously know a lot about horses, missie,' he said.

'I know everything there is to know about Mylor.'

'So you'd know if he was a machine?'

'A machine?' Angel put on her little-girl-lost face.

'He's genuine,' the security man advanced. 'I'm sure of it.'

The stable manager nodded. He smiled at Boff and said, 'I bet there's a hidy-hole somewhere that allows you to climb in and operate him.'

Boff blinked, looked nervously at me.

'You mean the chest-hatch,' I said, grinning. 'Don't crouch down or you might see the join.'

He laughed heartily. 'Kids with imagination,' he muttered. 'What it is to be young.'

'Yes, indeed.' There was a noticeable broadening of the Professor's smile.

The stable manager wrote 'OK' against Mylor's name on the clipboard. The two men strode towards Alaric's box.

'Gosh, that was close,' Angel breathed unevenly through parted lips.

'Well done, Roger,' the Professor said.

'He – he thought you were bluffing,' the tense, taut strain eased from Boff's face. 'Y-you nearly gave me a heart attack when you mentioned the chest-hatch, but by crikey, it worked.'

I grinned wryly. My own heart had missed a couple of beats, too.

Most of the horses had left for the saddling boxes. The Professor snatched a glance at his pocket-watch and instructed Angel to cover Mylor with his travelling-sheet. It was blue with red piping and embroidered with the Professor's initials. Our big stallion looked quite the aristocrat as he was led briskly back to his box.

'Well...' the Professor began, thumbing the forelock button and facing Boff and me. 'Well, now it's up to both of you. I've spent ten years dreaming of this moment and finally it's arrived. Whatever the outcome, I want you to know I'm proud of you. All of you.'

I lowered the chest-hatch. 'We'll win,' I promised him.

Angel's eyes were bright as she attached the identification arm-band to the left sleeve of her windcheater. It was printed with Mylor's name and number and would be displayed to the spectators as she walked our horse around the paddock.

I climbed inside, settled in the front seat, and switched on the solar-power. The chest-hatch hissed as Boff hauled it shut. He was behind me in an instant. I heard the snap of his safety harness and did likewise. The dials gleamed at me like a cluster of stars. I engaged the pace-selector and nudged the throttle. We were on the move.

Alaric was now out of his box and objecting strenuously to being manhandled. The stable manager's clipboard was sent flying as the black horse's

157

hindquarters bulled into his side. Grogan was saying things like, 'sorry, sir, but 'e's thin-skinned, and, 'the journey from Devon's made 'im grouchy', but as we turned I glimpsed a little black bag resting on his wicker-basket of tack. I suspected that Alaric was behaving exactly as Grogan had intended, and that the bag had been deliberately programmed to aggravate and enrage the horse. Certainly the stable manager had had enough. Looking badly winded he stooped to pick up the clipboard and waved Alaric away. A slow, bony smile formed on Grogan's lips as he covered the horse with a travelling-sheet and collected the little black bag.

'Hello, Angel. Hello, Professor.' Ought's thin face creased in welcome as we reached the saddling boxes. He fondled Mylor's muzzle and added, 'Are Roger and Boff about?'

'They're ... er,' the Professor faltered.

'In the grandstand,' Angel said quickly. 'Making sure they get a good seat for the race.'

'Oh,' his eyes dropped, 'only I had something to tell them. I thought it might be important.'

'Important?'

'Something Rusty Grogan said about Mylor. It struck me as odd at the time, especially as he'd just put two hundred pounds to win on Alaric.'

'He's been gambling?' The Professor tut-tutted. 'That's strictly against the Institute's –' He cleared his throat, shifted uncomfortably. 'That man has broken every rule in the book.'

'What book?'

The Professor was about to reply but Angel beat him to it. 'The saddle and number cloths, Professor,' she said. 'Hadn't you better collect them from the weighing-room?'

'Collect...?' His eyebrows shot up. 'Of course I

must. Yes, yes indeed. It's all very confusing...' His voice tailed away as he loped off to join the other trainers.

'As I was saying,' Ought continued, 'Grogan put all this money on Alaric, yet he rated your horse's chance very highly. He'll go like a bomb was what he said. At three fifteen, Mylor will go like a bloomin' bomb.'

'So he will,' Angel patted Mylor's neck. 'He'll leave them all standing. He's big, beautiful, and –'

'He's the most powerful horse in the world,' Ought added with a grin.

Suddenly a thought struck me like a punch below the belt. I swung to Boff. 'Three fifteen,' I blurted. 'Grogan said three fifteen!'

'So?' He looked puzzled. 'That's the "off" for the National. That's when all the runners and riders ... Crikey!' His face froze in shock as he was stuck by the same thought.

My mind spun backwards, recalling the night Mylor had been damaged at Parkway. They'd ripped his circuits and planted something – something we'd never find in a million years, Ought had overheard them saying. If Grogan was to be taken at his word, then...

'A b-o-m-b.' Boff's breath hissed against my neck. 'It – it's been set for three fifteen. As the starting tape goes up we're ... we're going to explode!'

I leaned back in my seat, my muscles trembling, my body chilled with fear. I stared unblinkingly at the video screen and watched Professor Parkway trundle towards us clutching the saddle and number cloths. Girth buckles rattled as Angel eagerly tightened the tabs. The chest-hatch creaked a little under the pressure. Nowhere to run now. We were sealed like moths in a chrysalis.

'What are we going to do?' Boff asked in a low,

hoarse voice.

'I don't know . . .' I began hesitantly.

'It – it could be anywhere. There are a hundred and one places to hide a bomb.'

'Can you defuse it?'

'Maybe,' he looked at me in doubtful hesitation. 'Maybe I could. It depends on the mechanism but –' he sighed, pressed his face into his clenched fists. 'Heck, Roger, we've got to find the darned thing first.'

'C'mon, Mylor,' Angel's voice filtered from the dash speaker and interrupted my thoughts. 'Everyone's heading for the paddock. Your public awaits you.'

'Hell,' I murmured, touching the throttle and setting our big horse into motion. We eased gently forward, joining the queue on the slow march to the parade ring.

'There's the swine,' Boff stabbed a finger at the video and indicated Grogan. 'He's grinning at us, Roger. He's watching us with a sickly smirk on his lips.'

'He's confident all right,' I agreed. 'He's eliminated the four other machines and now he's waiting for us to explode. He knows that Doctor von Sternberg's home and dry.'

'Never!' Boff unhooked his safety harness and pulled a pencil-flash from his pocket. Silky ripples of light fluttered around the cockpit as he rummaged under seats, probing the dim corners.

Grogan led Alaric into the line. The big horse swished his tail impatiently, his black coat shining like wet liquorice. He was wearing blinkers and the snug-fitting hood enclosed the whole of his face. All you could see were those dark hostile eyes peering coldly through the twin holes in the fabric. He had the look of a medieval charger preparing to do battle.

'This is hopeless, Roger,' Boff's throat tightened as he trained the pencil-flash on his wrist-watch. 'It's like looking for a needle in a haystack and we're running out of time.'

Mylor's ear-mikes were picking up the excited chatter from the thousands of spectators. As we entered the paddock I flicked the scan-switch and watched the sea of faces sweep across the video. People packed against the white-painted rails, jostling each other in an effort to get a clear view of the forty-two runners. All those eyes staring at me from the video were really quite frightening. It was only the sound of Boff opening and closing the equipment cover hatches that reminded me I had far worse things to worry about.

He said through a sigh of frustration, 'There are so many panels and coverings I could spend a weekend turning Mylor upside down and still draw a blank.'

'That's it!' I shouted the words as something clicked in my brain.

'W-what?'

'You've just told me where the bomb is.'

'But all I said was I could spend a weekend –'

'Turning Mylor *upside down*. Think back to the tin mine when the lights fused. You were puzzled about the position of the inspection plate.'

'Of course!' It took maybe a second for the penny to drop then he slapped his forehead with his palm. 'It had been fitted incorrectly. The inspection ... You're a numskull, Boff Parkway. You're a dunderhead. If ever there was a chump then –' He stopped calling himself names, dropped on his haunches, and started unfastening the plate.

'Is it...?' I began.

'I can't see ... I...' He transferred the flashlight to his left hand and began delving into the inspection cavity with his right. 'There's something here – I can feel wires and some sort of cylinder. It's resting on the solar generator.'

'Will it explode if moved?'

He shook his head. 'If it had been fitted with a trembler it would have gone off long before now. Trouble is, I can't budge it.'

'Shall I set Mylor on instinct and lend you a hand?'

'Daren't risk it, Roger. He's not used to crowds. The noise might well make him bolt.'

He had a good point. The dash speaker was beginning to vibrate with the continuous hum of excitement being generated by the spectators. The tension outside was electrifying. The roving eye of a television camera mounted high on a platform was transmitting pictures to millions of armchair viewers. We'd made several circuits of the paddock and I knew it was only a matter of minutes before a bell would ring as a signal for us to stop, turn inwards and find our jockey. This was a vital time for me to be at the controls.

'It's moving,' Boff whispered, having enlisted the help of a pair of long-nosed pliers. 'I've prised it loose. Now if I can just...' I heard a slow scrape as it lifted. Boff rested for a moment, breathing hard.

The bell clanged. Horses began turning towards the centre of the ring. I swung Mylor right, tracking Angel as she led us across to Paul and the Professor.

'Got it,' Boff wiped his forehead on his arm and let out his breath in a long, soundless whistle. 'It's a hellishly big device. If this goes off it'll blow us to smithereens.'

I snatched a quick glance over my shoulder. Boff pushed his glasses higher on the bridge of his nose as he carefully inspected the canister. It was silvery grey in colour and shaped like a small vacuum flask.

Boff carefully inspected the canister. It was silvery grey in colour and several thick wires sprouted from the top to form loops.

Several thick wires sprouted from the top to form loops.

'Tamper with these,' Boff informed me, 'and we're dead ducks. Each wire is linked to the detonator and any attempt to remove them will result in an instant explosion.'

'Can you unscrew the bottom?'

'I could, but it'll be booby-trapped.'

'So . . . ?'

'I'll cut away part of the casing to expose the timing mechanism. If we can stop the clock then we're safe.'

He pulled a miniature hacksaw from his tool-wrap, stroked a couple of pencil marks a third of the way down the cylinder and applied the saw's fine cutting edge to the metal. Steel filings clung to his trousers as he held the casing between his knees. The rasp of the blade made me shudder. It was like chalk squeaking on a blackboard. I tried to blot out the noise by busying myself at the control console. I twiddled the cockpit ventilation control a little and operated the dead-stop mechanism as we drew level with Paul and Professor Parkway.

'Mylor's a credit to you,' Paul flashed Angel a grin. 'He's the best turned out horse in the paddock.'

Angel smiled and said thank you. Her hair wound in twin braids around her head glinted like spun gold as she adjusted Mylor's sheepskin nose-band. Professor Parkway looked on proudly. He was wearing his usual tweed suit with a spotless white shirt and a tie striped like Neapolitan ice-cream.

The centre of the ring was packed with people. Clusters of owners, trainers and jockeys stood grouped around their respective horses exchanging last minute comments and instructions. I could see Major Palmer talking to Charlie Carver. Ought was steadying Alaric while Grogan's knuckly fingers tightened the girths on the electronic saddle. Doctor von Sternberg's eyes drifted from horse to horse and finally settled on Mylor. He brushed up the ends of his moustache, clamped his hands behind his back and walked towards us with long, purposeful strides.

'Ich freue mich Sie kennen zu lernen, Herr Professor,' he said, offering his hand in a gesture of friendship.

The Professor ignored the hand. 'I wish I could say the same,' he replied stiffly, 'but I refuse to exchange pleasantries with a man who will resort to the foulest of methods in order to further his own ends.'

'What's going on?' Boff looked up. The hacksaw stopped rasping.

'Von Sternberg's trying to be nice,' I said. 'He's just told the Professor how delighted he is to meet him.'

'Swine,' Boff muttered, turning his attentions back to the canister. 'I hope Gramps tells him to go suck a lemon.'

'You're an out-and-out scoundrel, sir,' the Professor was saying. 'Please step away from Mylor before I have you seen off by a Ring Steward.'

The Doctor's jaws snapped together and his head came forward. 'In less than fifteen minutes, Herr Professor, ze innards of your precious Mylor will be reduced to dust. I will leave you with zat thought.' He raised his Tyrolean hat, smiled crookedly at Angel and patted her head. 'Welch ein süsses, kleines Mädchen,' he added.

'Pardon?' Angel frowned.

'Er ... how you say in Engleesh ...?'

'What a sweet little girl,' the Professor translated.

'I'm not sweet,' Angel objected. 'I'm really quite sour. Pat my head again and I'll kick you hard in the shins.'

Von Sternberg's mouth hardened under the dark moustache. 'Viel Glück,' he muttered nastily, and departed.

'What was all that about?' Paul looked confused as he gripped the saddle.

'He was wishing us good luck,' the Professor said, giving the jockey a leg-up.

'No before – that bit about Mylor's innards being reduced to dust.'

'Haven't a clue, my boy. The man talks in riddles, yes indeed.'

'His Engleesh is not good,' Angel mimicked. 'And neither is his grotty old horse – Mylor's going to prove that.'

The cockpit shook slightly as Paul landed with a thump in the saddle. Boff gripped the canister tightly. He'd made two cuts in the metal and was now levering back a section of the casing. His pencil-flash inspected the interior. He whistled softly but said nothing. I didn't speak either; partly because I didn't want to spoil his concentration, but mostly because I thought I might stammer and I didn't want him to know I was scared half to death.

Angel clicked her tongue and Paul's heels tapped Mylor's flanks. I inched the throttle forward, watching the Professor gradually disappear from the video as we joined the procession from the paddock to the course.

'How long have we got, Roger?' Boff's voice was barely a whisper.

'About twelve minutes,' I said. 'Can you . . .?'

'Sure.' He sounded confident, but in the dim reflection of the dashboard panel lights I could see tiny frown lines knitting themselves between his eyes. He began pulling lenghts of cotton-wool packing from the canister and carefully teased out a sealed glass tube filled with a colourless liquid. Three slender wires were attached to the tube. Red, green and white. 'The explosive is nitroglycerine,' he informed me. 'It's extremely dangerous, hence the padding. A slight jar or knock could be enough to set it off.'

'And the wires?' I asked queasily.

'Two are linked to the inset detonator. The third is a booby.'

'Do you know which is which?'

He tried to smile and achieved a feeble grin. 'That's what I've got to figure out. If I cut the booby by mistake then the thing will instantly explode.'

I swallowed, hardly daring to consider the thought. I kept Mylor on course as Angel paraded him in front of the stands. The commentator's voice crackled over the public-address system, announcing each of the forty-two runners in turn. The ear-mikes were blasted by rapturous cheering from the racegoers and my fingers felt sticky on the T-shaped steering grips as each precious minute ticked away.

The horses in front of us were being turned and released by their lads. I caught a glimpse of von Sternberg's gold and black hooped colours as Charlie Carver cantered past us on Alaric. He was wearing very dark goggles which made it impossible to see his eyes, but the quirk on his lips told me he was laughing inwardly.

'You can beat him,' Angel murmured, pressing her face lovingly against Mylor's muzzle. She released the bridle and looked at Paul. Her voice was tight as she added, 'Please bring him back safely. He's so beautiful and I do love him so very, very much.'

'I'm pretty fond of him too,' Paul replied. 'There's nothing to fret about. Just you be there to lead him into the winners' enclosure.'

If only he knew he was sitting on a time-bomb, I

thought, pushing the pace-selector to 'canter' in response to his heels. We thundered back past the stands and across the Melling Road to the first fence. It was a normal formality of the Grand National to let your horse have a look at the kind of obstacle he'd have to jump, so we joined the other runners who were sniffing and peering at the tall spruce-dressed wall.

'Hold Mylor still,' Boff breathed, 'I'm cutting the green wire.'

I tensed. 'Are you sure...?'

The pliers snipped the wire. 'I'm sure,' he said.

My breath gushed out. 'Now which? The red or the white?'

'I don't know. I – I just don't know.'

'And if you cut the booby –'

'Then we go off bang. It's a toss up, Roger. A fifty-fifty chance. How much time have we left?'

'Less than five minutes.'

'It's hopeless,' he shook his head slowly, slackly. 'The clock's against us. We'll just have to make a choice.'

My mind raced. 'You're the boffin,' I said, 'so you make the choice. I know nothing about bombs. Your decision has to be better than me taking a stab at a colour.'

He took a few seconds off for thought, then said, 'I've a hunch the white wire's the booby.'

'Which means you cut the red?'

He nodded.

'Then do it. I trust your judgement.'

He lifted the pliers but stopped as Paul's verbal commands echoed from the dash speaker. The horses were leaving the fence for the starting tapes and Paul was getting angry because Mylor wouldn't respond.

'Hold it,' I ordered, fumbling for the throttle and

swinging Mylor round. 'Wait until we reach the tapes or your hand might slip.'

Boff held the canister tightly between his knees, the red wire looped around the forefinger of his left hand. He gripped the back of my seat in order to keep his balance. The safety harness would hamper his movements so he left it unfastened. It was three thirteen precisely as we arrived at the start.

The tapes were lowered. 'Okay, sort yourselves out,' the starter instructed.

One minute to the 'off'. There were no fixed positions so I eased Mylor into the centre of the straggly line of runners and quickly brought him to a halt.

Forty seconds. The pliers in Boff's hand opened. The red loop came towards the cutting edge.

'*Aagh!*' Boff screamed as Mylor suddenly lurched. The pliers rattled across the floor. Still clutching the canister he cannoned face first into the cockpit wall. I heard the tinkle of glass as his spectacles shattered.

'You damn idiot!' Paul was shouting at Charlie Carver. The jockey must have applied too much pressure to a stirrup because Alaric had swung crazily round and collided with Mylor's hindquarters.

Blood was pouring from Boff's nose. The shiny redness swam over his lips and down his chin in a torrent. He unhooked what was left of his spectacles and began raking the floor for the pliers.

The starter climbed his rostrum and the runners began easing forward. My hand hovered over the throttle, my heart banging in my ears.

'G-g-got them,' Boff croaked, gripping the pliers with quivering fingers.

'Cut the red!' I yelled.

'I – I can't see which ...'

The starter raised his white flag.

'*They're under starter's orders,*' the race commentator's voice boomed out.

'The red!' I yelled again. 'Cut the –' I stopped, stricken. *Both* wires were red. The glass tube was red. The canister was red. The device had been completely smothered in Boff's blood!

'I – I see it,' Boff squinted, hooked his finger under a wire. I braced myself for the worst as the pliers snipped it in two.

Nothing happened. We were safe. I breathed deeply, a breath that was almost a prayer.

'My hunch was right,' Boff said shakily. 'It *was* the red after all.'

As he removed his fingers from the cut wire he dragged some of the blood with them. I could see the plastic covering quite clearly. It was white.

The starting tapes lifted. I pushed the throttle forward as the loudspeaker announced, *'They're off!'*

Charlie Carver had unwittingly saved both our lives.

Chapter Ten

Mylor surged forward with the smoothness of an express train. Thirty fences to jump and four and a half miles to run. In less than ten minutes it would all be over.

Boff groped his way blindly to the rear of the cockpit. He fumbled the blanket from Spider's little box and carefully wrapped it around the glass tube of nitroglycerine. The liquid was still highly dangerous and it was vital to protect it against shock. I was very glad we'd left our cairn with a neighbour.

'Hold tight,' I warned, as the first fence loomed up on the video.

Boff gripped the third seat for all he was worth. Blood was still gushing from his nose and the sudden upward leap didn't help the problem. He began to cough and splutter and when he tried to speak he only succeeded in bringing forth an unintelligible croak. I waited until we'd touched down and then I wriggled a handkerchief from the pocket of my jeans. Boff took it gratefully as he settled behind me and fastened his safety harness.

Mylor was jumping like a dream. He was nicely tucked in behind the leaders and lying about eighth. Not that his position mattered at this stage of the race. All I had to do was blip the throttle and our chestnut wonder horse would kick dust in their faces as he surged to the front.

'H-how are we doing, Roger?' Boff spoke through the handkerchief, still trying to staunch the blood. 'Without my glasses I can't see a thing.'

'We're approaching Becher's Brook,' I told him. 'There's a riderless horse on our outside which could prove dodgy.'

'Where's Alaric?'

'No sign. I guess he's behind us.'

The speed-indicator needle began to climb as I increased acceleration. I was hoping to shake off the loose horse, but it increased its speed too, clinging to us like a limpet. A couple of the leaders had taken a tumble and I knew I was going to need all my wits about me in order to prevent Mylor from meeting the same fate.

Twenty yards ... fifteen ... ten ... The steering grips felt light and sensitive under my fingertips. I eased them back as the big fence filled the video. Mylor lifted, soared, flying, *alive*. We cleared it superbly, but the loose horse ploughed through the top and came down like a dive-bomber. I had to swerve on landing to avoid a collision and for a moment I thought we'd lost Paul. Certainly the saddle shifted and a string of swear words were picked up by the ear-mikes, but luckily the little splash of colour which swept across the video wasn't orange with black spots.

'The favourite's down,' I gasped, recognising the pattern of silks. 'That loose horse has caused a hell of a pile-up.'

Horses were thumping into the turf either side of us. I wrestled with the steering grips, guiding Mylor this way and that, dodging and weaving through the confusion of fallers and holding my breath until my lungs hurt.

'Are we clear?' Boff's knees pressed against my seat as he squinted at the video. 'All I can see is a rotten blur and even that's out of focus.'

'We're clear,' I affirmed, throttling back.

'Alaric?'

'Still no sign.'

'Let's hope he was brought down at Becher's.'

The loudspeaker commentary put paid to any chance of that: *'And with the field spread right across the course it's Indian Agent being pressed by Humble Manor and Calverley, then comes Mylor towards the outside, Diamond Edge towards the inside ... Rowlander is right up with the leaders and Alaric is making good progress...'*

'Damn!' Boff voiced his frustration.

I pressed a button on the dash and this illuminated a detailed map of the course. It was printed on dark celluloid, and as Mylor galloped so a thin beam of light plotted his position. The Canal Turn lay ahead of us. We jumped fence number eight faultlessly but a string of blinking red dots reminded me to switch Mylor to the inside of the track on the run to Anchor Bridge.

The fences came and went. Each horse in the race was represented on the celluloid map by a tiny green star. There had been forty-two at the beginning but now there were just twenty-six. The Chair, that colossal gorse barricade, wiped out another five. As the green stars vanished so the digital counter flashed the subtractions. The amount of fallers was frightening. We crossed the Melling Road on the second and final circuit with the field reduced to a third.

'What's that?' Boff's eyes were slits as he cocked his head at the video. 'One of the runners is moving up fast. It's going to overtake –'

'It's the TV crew,' I broke in. 'They're tracking the race with a camera mounted on a van.'

'Oh.' He swallowed, smiled sheepishly. 'Sorry.'

His face looked an awful mess. The bridge of his nose was the colour of an overripe plum and his nostrils were caked with dried blood. Whatever happened now, whatever the result, he'd remember this

Grand National long after the bruises had faded.

'That's my boy, that's my baby,' Paul whispered words of encouragement to Mylor as we sailed over the ditch for the second and final time.

There were two horses ahead of us, Diamond Edge and Rowlander. I pushed the throttle forward a notch and felt the power from the solar generator surge into Mylor's legs. The leaders appeared to be running at the limit of their strength and I thought that now would be a good time to get our horse up front.

Charlie Carver had similar ideas. I'd just piloted Mylor over the twentieth fence and was drawing well clear of Diamond Edge and Rowlander when suddenly Alaric's hooded face appeared at the corner of the video.

'I'm gonna bring you down at Becher's, Steel!' Carver shouted. 'There ain't no way you're gonna win this race!'

'Just you try it!' Paul yelled back.

A sly smile spread its tentacles around the corners of his wide mouth. 'I intend to,' he sneered. 'The only way you'll get past the winning post is by ambulance.'

Mylor and Alaric jumped the next fence neck and neck, flaring nostril to flaring nostril. There wasn't an inch between the two horses as they touched down.

'Increase power, Roger!' Boff gestured in exasperation. 'Carver intends to yank Paul out of the saddle. We've got to clear Becher's before him!'

Mylor lengthened his stride, responding smoothly to the pressure of my hand on the throttle. I opened it as far as I dared. The speed-indicator needle quivered just short of the red sector. We were going dangerously fast.

Four things happened next, and they happened so rapidly they were blurred into one movement. Carver powered Alaric forward to cover the gap, we lifted, he

Mylor and Alaric jumped the fence neck and neck, flaring nostril to flaring nostril. There wasn't an inch between the two horses as they touched down.

lifted, and there was this sharp crack as he sliced his racing whip viciously across Paul's face.

I gritted my teeth together and tensed all my muscles as Paul let out a cry of pain. Mylor landed awkwardly, his forelegs taking a punishing strain as our jockey slumped forward in the saddle. The steering grips vibrated under my fingers, emphasising our hopeless state of imbalance.

'Thug!' Boff exclaimed, clenching his elbows tight in front of him. 'If he wants to play dirty then we'll play dirty too. Switch on the solar-storage, Roger. We know it interferes with Alaric's circuits, so let's give Charlie Carver a taste of his own medicine.'

I nodded, flicked it down.

'Ha!' Boff began to chuckle. 'I bet he's going haywire – rearing like a bronco. That'll teach him, eh Roger?'

Boff's mental pictures in no way matched those being received by the video. Alaric remained calm and collected, and the gloating expression on Carver's hawklike face didn't change into one of terror.

'It's having no effect,' I said, jiggling the switch back and forth. 'Von Sternberg must have guessed we'd use it, so he's made modifications.'

'You mean Alaric *isn't* swerving?'

'He's cooler than a cucumber.'

'Blast!' Boff pulled a glum face.

Paul was shifting in the saddle above our heads. He was groaning a little but he'd taken his weight from the withers and was now more or less sitting upright. I reduced power, letting Alaric take the lead. We clung to the black horse's heels as he flipped over the next two fences and headed for Valentine's Brook.

'Carver's up to something,' I said. 'He's hanging back and glancing over his shoulder.'

'He wants us alongside,' Boff submitted. 'Go wide,

Roger, and keep your distance. We'll overtake him when we're good and ready.'

I turned away from Alaric and set Mylor on a track to the inside rail. Carver seemed to glare through his dark goggles as he too switched position. He arrowed in on us, his fingers curling eagerly around his whip ... waiting ... waiting...

Valentine's Brook heaved into sight.

Mylor lifted, stretched, white forelegs reaching skywards.

'No!' Paul's voice was desperate.

There was a sharp thwack as leather met human flesh. A stirrup iron was banging against Mylor's rib-cage. Carver laughed, the saddle moved violently, and I caught a glimpse of twirling ladybird silks as our jockey was thrown helplessly to the ground.

'Has Paul...?' The words choked in Boff's throat.

I opened my mouth and shut it again. The race commentator confirmed the worst: *'Mylor's unseated his rider at Valentine's ... that leaves Alaric a good six lengths clear of Diamond Edge ...'*

Boff buried his head in his hands. 'All for nothing,' he heaved a long pained sigh. 'That's the end of Gramps' dream.'

I thumped the top of the dash with my fist. I felt sick, saddened, cheated. Alaric was surging ahead, getting smaller and smaller on the video, and there wasn't anything we could do about it. Or was there? A thought suddenly struck me. I whirled on Boff.

'The Institute's rules,' I said sharply. 'Tell me exactly what the Professor has to do to gain member-ship.'

'You already know,' he murmured disinterestedly. 'We had to build a horse capable of winning the Grand National.'

'Any mention of a jockey?'

'No.' He frowned, pondered the question. 'But you can't win the race without one.'

'That depends on what you mean by "win". A riderless horse can't collect the prize money but it could still pass the post first.'

'Blister me!' He clenched his teeth, adding anxiously, 'Y-you mean Mylor could still do it? You mean the result wouldn't count with the racing officials but Gramps would still qualify for –'

'Institute membership, yes.'

His face lit up. 'I – I guess you're right.'

'I *am* right,' I said positively, pushing the throttle hard forward. 'Now let's get Alaric.'

There were two ditches and two fences left to jump. Our black quarry had a lead on us of ten lengths at least, but we were closing by the second. I hung on to the steering grips with grim determination, listening to Mylor's hooves as they drummed over the turf, a plan for revenge knitting itself together in my mind.

Charlie Carver jumped the fourth from home full of confidence. He must have been deafened by the cheering crowd because he didn't spot us until we drew level, and even then he had to be prompted by a warning from the race commentator. The words: '*Alaric's well clear but the loose horse, Mylor, could prove troublesome...*' floated from the loudspeakers.

'Get back you ruddy –' Carver's whip sliced brutally into Mylor's neck.

I flinched, but I heard Boff's small voice reminding me that Mylor couldn't feel pain.

'*Get back!*' Carver sounded desperate. The whip cracked again.

I heeled the steering grips hard over. Mylor's left shoulder smacked into Carver's right leg and wedged it tightly against Alaric's ribs. He struggled frantically to free it but the pressure was too great. His leg was pinned as surely as if it had been clamped in a vice.

'*No!*' He let out a thin bubble of a scream. We were fast approaching the ditch-fence before Anchor Bridge, and Charlie Carver was anticipating what would happen if he was prevented from kicking down on both stirrup irons.

I looked at the video and settled my breathing. I thought briefly about Paul. The ambulance following the runners would have picked him up by now. He'd be shaken and bruised and feeling pretty miserable.

The ditch loomed ahead. Carver was still squirming to free his leg but Mylor didn't yield an inch. I left it to the last possible moment before hauling back on the steering grips.

Carver's boot dragged across Mylor's chest, his flank, his stifle; the noise racketing into the cockpit as our horse stretched out his neck, flying like an angel. We spanned the ditch, just clearing the fence by a whisker.

'GAAAAHH!' Carver's cry burst from the dash speaker.

A shimmer of gold and black racing silks somersaulted across the video. The ear-mikes shook with the sound of tearing metal and the scrunching, snapping, thunderous roar of Alaric piling headlong into the fence.

Boff screwed up his face. 'Bloomin' heck,' he whispered. 'Von Sternberg'll hit the roof of the grandstand.'

'Ja, zat is good,' I mimicked.

'He'll be arrested when the stewards pick up Alaric's pieces.'

'I doubt it,' I grinned. 'If he's got any sense, he'll be heading back to Austria right now.'

Mylor flicked his heels over the last two fences and we turned into the straight. I felt a shiver of excitement as the noise swelled from the stands. The background was just a moving blur of faces. All cheering, shouting, waving...

But not for us. We were just a loose horse who'd finished the course without a rider. No, the applause was for Diamond Edge. I could see him on the celluloid map, a very tired green star wending his way home some fifty yards behind us. As we cruised past the winning post I found myself being glad that in spite of everything the result would be a fair one.

Professor Parkway and Angel were waiting for us by the gap in the rails. I pulled the throttle back, felt my weight lurch against the safety harness as Mylor decelerated. The needles drifted down off the dials.

'Well done, all of you. Well done indeed,' the Professor lit his pipe, his face bright with happiness. 'You had me worried for a moment ...' puff – puff '... thought you might give up when you lost Paul...' puff –puff '... didn't think you'd realise that with or without a jockey it still counted.'

'My beautiful, beautiful Mylor,' Angel sounded breathless as she unbuckled the girths and removed the saddle. 'The Professor's now a member of the most exclusive club in the world and he owes it all to you.'

Boff put his hands on my shoulders and squeezed. I didn't have to turn around. In the reflection of the dash instruments I could see his cheeks pushed back in a huge, dreamy smile.

'The boys must be tired.' Professor Parkway pointed towards the racecourse stables with the stem of his pipe. 'Let's get Mylor back to his box and then we can all go to the cafeteria for a nice cup of tea.'

About half of the runners had already arrived at their loose-boxes. These consisted of early fallers and horses who had found the four and a half mile slog just too much for them. Coats steamed and muscles trembled with fatigue as stable lads scurried to and fro. Lather was removed with sweat scrapers, saddle marks were erased by vigorous hand slapping, eyes and nostrils were cleaned with damp sponges, and any dried mud was brushed from delicate skins with a dandy and a considerable amount of elbow grease.

Angel led us into box number two and the Professor closed the split-door. I zeroed the switches and unclipped my safety harness. 'All systems at shutdown,' I announced.

Boff groped around the floor until he found the chest-hatch lever. I heard the familiar hiss as it slowly opened. I felt a little saddened because I knew I was hearing it for what was probably the last time.

'Good heavens above!' The Professor's face held an expression of frozen astonishment as Boff fumbled his way down the treads.

'An accident, Gramps,' he said bleakly. 'Mylor lurched and I wasn't strapped in, and –' He paused, cleared his tonsils. 'It's a heck of a long story.'

'A colourful one, too, judging by your face, yes indeed. Now let me see...' He began patting the pockets of his jacket. 'I'm sure I brought a spare pair of spectacles –'

'In the wicker basket with the first-aid kit,' Angel interrupted, undoing Mylor's throatlash and removing the bridle. 'I've got to pack the tack so shall I get them?'

'Excellent, young lady, excellent.'

Boff closed the chest-hatch and I thumbed the forelock button. Mylor bent his long neck and butted his head playfully against my chest as life surged into his instinct circuits. I stood silently fondling his ears. The climax was over and that meant that the holiday was also over. I was suddenly feeling quite glum.

'You're looking very down in the mouth, my boy,' the Professor remarked. 'This isn't a time for long faces, this is a time for celebration and smiles.'

'What will happen to Mylor?' I asked vaguely.

'Happen?'

'After we leave.' I lifted my eyes. 'Promise me he won't end up like Noble Ransom.'

He frowned.

'Scrap metal,' I reminded him. 'You once said that about the Count de Chartres' horse and it made my blood run cold.'

He seemed genuinely amused as he raised his wispy eyebrows. 'That was just a figure of speech, Roger,' he assured me. 'Mylor's as much a part of Parkway Grange as the mazemobile and I shall expect you and Angel to visit him often – in fact I'm relying on it. A Grand National horse must have plenty of exercise, yes indeed. How are you fixed for the summer holidays?'

My heart gave a great throb of joy. 'We're not,' I said. 'Can we...?'

'Of course, my boy. Delighted to have you.'

'Delighted to have Angel's cooking, too, eh Gramps?' Boff grinned knowingly.

'Er ... well ... I ...'

Mylor scraped a hoof across the box floor and whinnied in agreement.

The Professor pretended to be angry. 'Stop taking sides,' he said, wagging a finger at Mylor. 'Your circuits are getting a little too sharp. I think I'll have to moderate your electronic sensitiser, yes indeed.'

Boff smiled expansively and patted Mylor's neck. I glanced at my watch and was about to suggest that we tried to find Paul when the box door gave a rending creak. Angel almost fell inside. Her cheeks had lost their colour, and the fear in her eyes told me that something had driven her to instant panic.

'Grogan!' It came out explosively. 'He – he's on

the construction site ... try-trying to start the bull-dozer. Oh, Roger, he's going to destroy Mylor!'

Boff took the spectacles from her trembling hands and hooked them behind his ears. 'He wouldn't,' he gulped. 'He'd have to be off his nut to –'

'Listen!' I broke in. 'I think...'

There was a throaty chug of an engine, a careless grinding of gears. Fear twisted in my stomach as the ground began to shudder and the locks on the box door rattled in their keepers. Mylor's ears pricked forward, his nostrils flaring, as if he could sense the impending danger.

'What the hell's going on?' a voice shouted.

'Some bloke's moving the bulldozer,' another voice replied. 'Hey, cut that out, mate, – you're scaring my horse to beggary!'

Several cries now. Confusion among the stable lads. Shouts of, 'Whoa! Whoa!' as the revving of the bull-dozer grew louder and horses began skittering in panic.

'Get your nags in their boxes and keep 'em teth-ered!' Grogan ordered harshly. 'I'm only after the animal in box number two!'

We all stiffened. I pushed open the top half of the split-door and peered out on the bright yellow mon-ster as it rumbled slowly towards us. The exhaust sprouted from the bonnet like a submarine's peri-scope, polluting the air as it coughed out a haze of diesel vapour. Grogan sat at the controls, his skin grey, waxy, and filmed with sweat. His eyes were wild, with a distant, fixed stare that terrified me. I watched his feet pump the pedals, his hands move jerkily on the power levers. The tank-like tracks bit into the tarmac, throwing up swirls of dust as they crept stealthily forward.

'Send Mylor out!' Grogan yelled. 'Send him out

now – or I'm gonna demolish that loose-box!'

Angel looked pleadingly at the Professor. She drew a long breath and clutched at his arm. 'P-please,' she blurted. 'You can't let him ... he – he'll be torn to pieces.'

The Professor hesitated, looking first at Mylor and then at the bulldozer.

'Grogan'll ram us, Gramps,' Boff said. 'He's scatty enough to do anything.'

'*No!*' Angel threw her arms around Mylor's neck and hugged him close. 'I won't let you send him out there. I won't let you destroy him. He can't win against a bulldozer...' Her voice choked and she swung desperately to me. 'Tell them Roger ... tell them they mustn't –'

'C'mon Prof!' Grogan cut her off. 'Ten seconds for Mylor to come out, or else I'm comin' in!'

There was a brutal sneer of satisfaction on his face as he pulled the lever that operated the mechanical shovel. The drive whined and the ripper-edges shaped like huge teeth lifted. They were levelled menacingly at us, the sun glinting on their shiny steel surface.

'Wait,' the Professor raised a hand. 'Let's talk this over calmly, like two rational human beings.'

Grogan's eyes widened, then narrowed. He said through clamped teeth, 'I ain't feelin' very rational, Prof. I staked a wad of notes on Alaric winning the National and I should've been leavin' 'ere with me pockets bulging full of money. I'm after revenge. Me own brand of justice for what you done to Charlie and me.'

'So you propose to damage Mylor?'

'Damage 'im?' He laughed harshly. 'I don't propose to damage 'im, Prof. *I propose to rip him into shreds and trample him into the dust!*'

184

'You swine!' Boff retaliated. 'You're not a man, you're the lowest form of scum.'

'Shut your face, four-eyes,' Grogan snapped, 'or I might be tempted to go for you instead of the 'orse.'

I looked left and right, my eyes searching for support. There wasn't any. All the lads and horses had hastily taken cover in their loose-boxes and the area appeared deserted.

'Five seconds, Prof!' Grogan began revving the bulldozer.

Angel clung a little tighter to Mylor. Our big stallion's muscles started to quiver. His soft liquid eyes were pinned unblinkingly upon the mechanical shovel, as though he was mentally weighing it up, classifying it as a mistrustful and dangerous beast.

'I think he's bluffing,' I stated. 'He wouldn't dare ram a box full of people.'

'Of course he wouldn't,' Angel agreed, relaxing slightly.

'Algernon?' The Professor looked at Boff.

'I think he's screwy enough to do it,' Boff said gravely, 'but I'm no coward, so I say we all stick together.' His voice was tight as he added, 'Besides, he shouldn't have called me four-eyes.'

'Time's run out, Prof!' Grogan's cold warning speared the air. 'Now are you lettin' the 'orse out – or am I comin in to get 'im?'

Mylor snorted, swished his tail.

'Take it easy, boy,' I whispered.

The Professor put on a brave face, but his voice when it came was thin and quavery. 'Do your worst, Mr Grogan,' he said. 'I haven't devoted ten years of my life building Mylor in order to desert him when I'm confronted by a melodramatic fool.'

Grogan's lips twisted and he spat angrily at the tarmac. His hand reaching for the power shift lever was the last thing I saw. Professor Parkway closed and bolted both halves of the door and ordered us all to the back of the loose-box.

'Well, we've called his bluff,' he announced softly. 'I only hope...' His words petered out into silence as the bulldozer's engine began rising in pitch.

Our faces were close. We looked at each other too terrified to speak.

The treads rumbled nearer, crawling, hugging the ground.

I bit into my lip and clamped my hands over my ears, trying to block out the crescendo of sound. Grogan hadn't been bluffing. *He wasn't going to stop!*

Mylor whinnied shrilly. He shied away from the noise but as Angel went to catch hold of his mane he bucked and pitched himself muscularly at the box door. His white forefeet hammered the timbers, smashing them like balsa wood, kicking the bolts from their keepers. In less than a second, his concentrated energy had almost reduced the door to sawdust. He bored an exit, trampling over the shredded wood splinters that littered the ground.

'Zoot!' Angel's body jerked erect.

Through the ragged hole I could see Grogan's incredulous, startled face. He fumbled with the gear-shift and selected reverse. The ripper teeth of the mechanical shovel began backing away. We were out of danger.

'Keep still!' he yelled, his feet working furiously on the pedals as Mylor taunted him, dodging this way and that, but all the time drawing the bulldozer further and further away from us. 'Keep still, you brainless donkey. I'm gonna tear you limb from limb!'

Mylor shook his flaxen mane and extended his nostrils. The crude shape of the bulldozer emphasised the strength and sheer perfection of his body, sculpturing the contours. The muscles rippled in his quarters as once again the shovel lunged, and once again Mylor ducked away.

'He can't keep this up,' Boff remarked, the paleness of his face suddenly taking on a yellow tinge. 'The race, busting out of the box like that – his solar energy must virtually be at zero.'

He *was* getting weaker. I held my breath as the bulldozer juddered into a sideways slide and the ripper edges slashed murderously close to Mylor's neck. The Professor gasped, and Angel flung her hand against her mouth to stifle a scream.

'W-what are we going to do, Gramps?' Boff croaked. 'Th – the zinc-air batteries are failing fast.'

The Professor gestured helplessly.

'I know what *I'm* going to do,' Angel stepped from the broken door and pulled a headcollar and lead rein from the basket of tack. 'I'm going to get him away from Grogan before –'

'You'll do no such thing!' The Professor's voice went up an octave. 'I'm responsible for your safety and I absolutely forbid...'

She wasn't listening. She'd turned her back on us and was already sprinting determinedly towards Mylor.

Grogan saw her – saw the tack in her hand – and immediately swung the bulldozer away from the horse and into her path. Whether he really meant to run her down or just frighten her was anybody's guess. The next couple of seconds were a confused mixture of action and sound.

Angel let out a little cry of pain as her madly dashing feet tangled with the lead rein. She was sent sprawling only yards from the advancing bulldozer's tracks.

Mylor stood quite still, ears lying flat, neck stretched

aggressively forward. He seemed to be watching the ever-diminishing gap between Angel and the bright yellow machine. Grogan had a maniac gleam in his eyes and he was cursing freely. He looked briefly towards the Professor and shouted, 'Which is it to be, Prof, the 'orse or the kid?'

'Not my sister!' I burst out, edging forward.

The Professor gripped my arm.

'Move, Angel, move!' Boff yelled.

'I can't ... My ankle...' She winced painfully as she tried to stand.

The tracks nibbled away the inches. Angel's face froze in terror as the shovel's wicked looking teeth passed slowly over her head.

'*Help me-e-e-e!*'

Mylor's hooves clattered on the tarmac. Sparks flew from his shoes as he lunged forward in a bid to protect Angel. He took the full weight of the ripper edges against his side, and they struck him with crushing force.

The bulldozer stopped, shuddered, its tracks gouging into the tarmac with furious jerks. Mylor showed every tortured muscle as he fought against the strain. Grogan increased revs and the engine screamed. The tracks whirred frantically, churning up dust and grit, but Mylor didn't lose his footing. He stood bravely taking the strain, his body now beginning to shake uncontrollably with the effects of this savage punishment.

Boff turned to me, alarm, flaring in his eyes. 'C-cripes, Roger!' he exclaimed. 'We didn't remove the nitro–'

A hollow, muffled *BOOM* rocked Mylor. His body stiffened for what seemed like an eternal moment, and then his neck fell limply forward.

I closed my eyes for a fraction of a second and when